SC
PL

I SWEAR

Lane Davis

SIMON & SCHUSTER BFYR

NEW YORK LONDON TORONTO SYDNEY NEW DELHI

An imprint of Simon & Schuster Children's Publishing Division
1230 Avenue of the Americas, New York, New York 10020

Book design by Hilary Zarycky
The text for this book is set in Electra.
Manufactured in the United States of America
2 4 6 8 10 9 7 5 3 1
Library of Congress Cataloging-in-Publication Data
Davis, Lane.
I swear / Lane Davis.
p. cm.
Summary: "After Leslie Gatlin kills herself,
her bullies reflect on how things got so far"— Provided by publisher.
ISBN 978-1-4424-3506-3 (hardback)
[1. Bullying—Fiction. 2. Suicide—Fiction.] I. Title.
PZ7.D29454Iam 2012
[Fic]—dc23
2011046310
ISBN 978-1-4424-3508-7 (eBook)

For E.K.B., who loved this story first

—L.D.

I SWEAR

PROLOGUE

Leslie Gatlin couldn't believe the words she was reading on the screen.

Of all the emails and all the Facebook messages and all the texts and phone calls she'd received since she'd stepped into Macie Merrick's crosshairs, this one was the worst.

As the sobs came one more time, she slowly closed the lid of her silver laptop and laid her head down on top of it.

You finally did it. You finally lost the last friend you'll ever have.

It was almost a relief. No one would miss her now when she left.

She picked up her laptop. The necklace Jake had brought her was lying on the coffee table, and she slipped it into the back pocket of her jeans. She walked across the living room to the front entry foyer and paused there for a moment, staring up at the modern chandelier that hung from the ceiling two stories above. It was pretty, but unremarkable, sort of exactly what you'd expect. The tile was hard and cool against her bare feet, and as she reached the stairs to her room, her toes sank into the new carpet: beige and soft—a nice camel-color berber—durable, strong, and above all, neutral.

"It'll go so nicely with nearly any decorating scheme," her mother always said when she put this same carpet in yet another stairway in yet another remodel in yet another neighborhood.

"Flip a house a year" had been her father's real estate investment plan, and it had worked like a charm. He was a contractor; her mother was a real estate agent with a flair for interior design.

So for the past six years, Leslie had lived in a newly remodeled house each school year. Every one was different, but every one was exactly the same: eggshell walls, bone ceilings, café au lait trim, camel berber carpet on the stairs. It all looked tan to Leslie.

"It's like we live in Banana Republic," she always told her mother as she pleaded for an accent wall to liven up her bedroom in each new house. She begged for pink in sixth grade, then purple in seventh. Finally she asked for a warm olive green in eighth, but the answer was always the same:

"We'll be moving soon, and deep colors are so hard to hide with white."

Since sixth grade she'd lived in houses decorated for the people who would live there next.

She opened the door to her room and suddenly wondered who that would be.

Who will live in these four white walls after I do? Who will call this home?

Her dad had already signed a contract on the next remodel. Her mom had the For Sale sign in the garage. It had taken longer to secure the financing now that the housing market had tanked, but her parents were going to do well on this house, just like they'd done well on all the others.

She placed her laptop on her desk, and as she closed the door to her room, she reached up and took down the sign that was hanging there. "LESLIE" was spelled out in a lumpy font of macaroni and spray paint—a camp craft that her mother insisted on installing in every new house. Leslie fingered the petrified pasta covered in glitter and dust and thought about the summer after third grade, when she'd made friends with the twins, long before they'd started going to school together.

Suddenly she was crying again.

She felt for the necklace in her back pocket, and before she could stop herself, she'd taken it out and put it on, pulling open the neck of her zip-up sweater in front of the full-length mirror that leaned against the wall next to her bed so she could see the tiny silver anchor hanging under her chin. Jake had worn the ship, and Jillian the little captain's wheel. She stared back at her reflection for a moment, then glanced away as if it hurt to look too long.

In order to combat the glare of the white walls, she'd hung as many bulletin boards and tack strips as her dad would put up for her, and pinned up pictures from magazines and catalogs along with shots she'd enlarged and printed from her camera. Vacation with her parents rafting in the Grand Canyon last summer, ads from the *Seventeen* prom dress issue, pages from the spring J.Crew catalog.

Her eyes wandered from the mirror to a picture of her and Jillian and Jake on a sailboat the summer after eighth grade, when they'd bought the necklaces. Their families had gone to Cape Cod that year. There had been sailing, and lobster on the beach, and races in the sand, and one night, when no one else was awake, a kiss from Jake.

She slowly reached up and took down the picture. She ran her fingers across the smiles in the shot—the windblown hair, the handsome cleft in Jake's chin, Jillian's hazel eyes, the surf and the sky behind them. She laid the photo gently in the top of the duffel bag that was packed and sitting on her bed. She zipped it closed, then picked it up and slowly turned around the room, fingering the anchor at her neck.

Just get in the car.

She'd been considering it for months. Finally, tonight, the pain was too great, and she'd made the decision to leave.

Just get in the car.

She'd repeated this like a mantra. Whatever it took to get her to the garage, to get her to the car, to get her out of here.

Earlier that night she'd been gathering the things she wanted to take with her, when Jake had showed up on the front porch, holding her necklace. Demanding to know how Macie Merrick had gotten her hands on it.

"Where are you going?" he'd asked.

"Portland," she'd lied. "To stay with my aunt Laura."

"That's all you're taking?" The bag in her hand had been small and light.

"I won't need anything else."

Now she switched off the light and padded back down the stairs to the kitchen. In the glow of the screen on the front of the silver refrigerator her father installed in every kitchen he built, Leslie found the spare key to her mom's car in the drawer under the toaster.

In the garage, she tossed the duffel bag onto the passenger seat of her mother's Audi, put on her seat belt, adjusted the mirrors, and turned the key in the ignition. She knew her parents would never hear the car start from the opposite end of the house, and as she turned it on, the oldies station her mother listened to softly filled the air. The music swelled and a woman with a sob in her voice sang out the words "All I see is you."

She rolled down the windows, and the warmth of the garage rolled into the car. It was late April, but already the temperatures were headed up, and the garage smell of cement and unfinished Sheetrock and new spackling filled her nose. Leslie listened to the song and wondered who this woman was and where her love had gone. Or maybe this singer had left like Leslie was doing now.

She picked up the duffel bag on the passenger seat and laid it on her lap. She felt the anchor around her neck and considered where to go. She looked up at the rearview mirror and caught a glimpse of herself: A girl with chin-length blond hair whose mascara was running stared back at her. Perhaps once, she'd been pretty. Now she was unremarkable, sort of exactly what you'd expect.

Tears started to stream down the face of the girl in the mirror, and as they did, Leslie closed her eyes. The words she'd heard so often rang in her ears.

You are pathetic and worthless. You should just kill yourself.

In her heart, Leslie felt something click. Like a door swinging closed. She finally knew one thing for sure: Even if she went to Portland, even if she drove a hundred miles an hour and didn't stop until she was standing on Aunt Laura's doorstep, she could never outrun this pain. It would never end, unless she ended it.

Right now.

Deep down inside, she knew that going to Aunt Laura's would never do that. That was just the story she'd told herself to get her to the car in the garage. Going nowhere was the only real option. It had been her first idea, and now in the warmth of the garage, with the sound of the softly purring engine and the song filling her ears, she decided it had been her best choice. In the end, it was the least complicated, and the only thing that would work for certain.

As the exhaust began to tickle her nose, she laid her head back against the seat and closed her eyes. Her hand wandered to the shoulder strap of the duffel bag in her lap. She took a long, deep breath and thought about all the things she'd packed to bring along.

And all the things she'd leave behind.

1. JILLIAN

When I got back to my room with the Diet Cokes, Macie was finishing the Facebook message to Leslie. As I set the cans down on the desk, she looked up at me with a quick smirk, then back at the screen. A satisfied smile slowly spread across her face. Then she flipped a long strand of honey-blond hair over her shoulder.

"Straight-A Jillian, your proofreading skills are now required. Nothing is worse than a typo in a suicide note."

"Totally." Krista giggled. "That would really make you want to kill yourself." She and Beth dissolved into laughter on the floor. I gingerly stepped over Katherine to sit down at the computer as Macie slid away and popped open a Diet.

The words on the screen were typed into a Facebook message. It read:

TOP 10 THINGS TO REMEMBER IN YOUR SUICIDE NOTE

1. Apologize for all the terrible sweaters you wore.
2. A brief rundown of how bad you were at volleyball.
3. How much it hurt that your daddy was never home enough.
4. Tell everyone how sorry you are that you won't be at prom this year, so someone else will have to be "worst dressed."
5. A thank-you to all your best girlfriends, who were so nice to you. (Oh. Wait. There weren't any because you were a slut who stole people's boyfriends.)
6. Who you're leaving all your craptastic earrings to.
7. How sad you were that your boobs never grew in.
8. A line from one of those stupid country songs you listened to.
9. Why we shouldn't be sad now that you're gone. (Not that we would be.)
10. Tell Jake how you're doing this for him so that he won't have ugly babies.

"Is 'craptastic' a word?" I asked.

"Oh, who cares? It's not like she's clever enough to use a word like that in a book report, let alone a suicide note." Macie was very pleased with herself. I could tell that this week at school would be easier. She'd been begging for a sleepover since last Monday. Finally, I'd invented a chemistry exam that required a study group so my mom would buy into a Sunday-night slumber party. Now if we could just get this message sent before Jake got home, we'd be set.

"Looks good," I said. "Our weekly missive appears to be ready."

"Oh, Beeeeeth . . . ," trilled Macie. It was a silly tradition that we'd established. Macie typed, I proofread, Beth pressed send every week.

"Ta-*da*!" squealed Beth, the tiny gymnast in our midst, who jumped in a single fluid motion from the floor to the chair at the computer desk, somehow joining me on a seat I didn't realize had room for the both of us.

She clicked.

She clapped.

And as she turned around, the door to my room swung open with such force that it bounced against the wall and knocked the lamp off my dresser. Krista screamed as the bulb flashed purple and burned out. Suddenly, all six feet, two inches of my twin brother, Jake, were standing in the doorway.

"Where did you get this?" he asked. His voice was so still, no one dared to breathe. There was no air left in the room.

I tried to act nonchalant. I squinted at the silver chain dangling from his fist as if I couldn't quite make out what he was holding, as if I didn't know.

But I knew. We all did. And Jake's knuckles were white.

Katherine was typically the quiet one, but she must've noticed me flinch under Jake's gaze, because she was the only one to jump in.

"What is that?" she asked, sitting up on the knees of her plaid pajama pants and reaching for the anchor dangling from the chain in Jake's hand.

Without moving his eyes from mine, he pulled the chain out of her reach as a cloud crossed his clear blue eyes.

"Jills, you know exactly what it is," he said.

The short sleeve of Jake's green polo strained against the biceps of his right arm as he gripped the necklace. The pendant trembled on the chain from the tension in his hand. His whole body was on a slow boil.

"Dang, Jake." Macie whistled. "You're so sexy when you're angry."

For one moment, Jake's eyes left me and fixed on Macie in a look of such contempt that even Macie withered backward from the heat.

"Don't ever speak to me again," he spat at her so slowly it felt like the words were separate explosions from an armful of hand grenades he'd lobbed into each corner of the room. "I want you out of my life."

Then he turned on his heel and headed back down the hall.

I'll never forget how we sat there in silence for what seemed like an eternity as we listened to the front door slam, then the car door, then heard Jake squeal away from the curb. I didn't realize it then, but that was the moment it all began—or it all ended, depending on your point of view, I suppose. In the span of time between his tires peeling out and Krista's next giggle, I sat in the eerie quiet and understood two things:

I didn't know exactly how we'd gotten here.

But I knew exactly where Jake was going.

2. KATHERINE

I knew Leslie was dead before I opened my eyes. It was Beth's crying that woke me up, and my very first thought was *Leslie's gone and killed herself.* As I lay there listening to Beth cry, I felt that familiar knot in the pit of my stomach. It's the same one I got the day we left Atlanta almost two years ago. I had cried that day while I was hugging my old aunt Liza good-bye.

"No use crying when life hands you different cards than the ones you wanted," Aunt Liza always said when I was little. "Besides, if you show folks your hand by the look on your face, they'll call your bluff."

I lay as still as I could on the pull-out couch in the corner of the TV room in Jillian's huge upstairs suite and listened for clues. Krista tried to comfort Beth on the edge of the air mattress across the room.

"Beth, it's okay," she said.

"No, Krista, it's not okay. This is not okay."

I heard a rustling as Jillian jumped up and closed the door of the TV room all the way. "You guys, we have to keep it down."

"Keep what down?" Beth was crying so hard that she could barely choke out the words. "This isn't a secret, Jillian. It's all over Facebook."

Beth was sobbing too loudly to ignore, and even though I didn't want to, I opened my eyes and sat up. They had forgotten I was there, because Jillian jumped about three feet in the air, and Beth stopped crying for a second.

"Leslie is dead, isn't she?" I said.

No one moved for what seemed like an eternity. I realized later that this was the first time any of us had said the word "dead." For some reason, saying it out loud made it real. The word hung there in midair and I wished that someone, anyone, would grab it and hide it, or hurl it out the upstairs window into the pool out back. Instead it tumbled end over end with a gathering velocity, like a frigid wave, and as it crashed over us, Macie walked into the room from the bathroom that Jillian shared with Jake.

Macie was showered and dressed and looked like she'd stepped out of the window at the Barneys in Pacific Place. Her dark-blond hair was perfect and framed her face in long, shiny layers.

"Yes, Katherine. Leslie killed herself. She died last night huffing exhaust in her own garage."

Macie took a box of tissues from a shelf next to the television and handed it to Krista.

"Beth, darling, when you dry your eyes, feel free to leave a post on Leslie's Facebook page along with the hundred and seventeen of us who have already done so. I can't help but think that our true sympathy should go to her parents, though. I simply can't imagine how anyone could be so selfish."

She turned around and fished a small zippered pouch from her Louis Vuitton overnight bag on the floor. She produced two diamond stud earrings, which she put in as she made her way to the full-length mirror next to the couch, where I was sitting. She narrowed her eyes as she surveyed her own reflection. When no one spoke or moved, she suddenly turned and looked at each of us in turn.

"What?" she asked.

Beth grabbed a tissue and blew her nose. Jillian looked at me; Macie followed her gaze and smiled.

"I know it's only seven, but you need to look alive, VP. You're going to want to join me at school early this morning. There may be news crews. This sort of stuff is a local anchor's wet dream. Dress for the cameras."

She picked up her bag and headed toward the hallway. When she reached the door of Jillian's suite, she turned back toward Jillian and frowned.

"I don't know what Jake's issue was last night," she said, "but I know I can count on you, right, Jillian?"

There was a tense silence, and I watched as Jillian sputtered and blushed under the heat of Macie's gaze.

"Wha—? Yes, I mean, yeah. Of course," she choked out.

Macie nodded once. Then she was gone.

Jillian glanced over at me as I stood up and walked toward the bathroom. I shook my head and smiled at her, then rolled my eyes after Macie with a little sigh. Jillian almost smiled at me, and took a deep breath—the first one I'd seen her take since I sat up and opened my eyes. Her relief was like the wiggle of the catfish my grandpa used to take off my fishing line and toss back into the water at the pond out behind his house during the summer when I was little.

You can always read Jillian's cards. That girl's face is a full house.

3. BETH

By the time I got to school my eyes were so red and puffy from crying that they were almost swollen shut. I looked like Mary Alice Splinter that day in eighth grade when she bobbled her approach on the springboard and smacked the vault with her forehead. It was the last practice before the winter invitational, and Mary Alice was our strongest all-around competitor. I remember watching her hold her head and wail into the mats. I stood there, helpless, while the coaches tended to her. The worst part of all was the sickening feeling that we'd already lost before we'd had the chance to compete—like everything was over before it ever started.

I remember feeling helpless as I stood there watching life buzz by around me. All the other girls seemed to know what to do. One went to the school office to get a secretary to call

Mary Alice's mom. Two more went to her locker to get her things. Another helped the coaches apply cold packs and talk to Mary Alice while we waited for the ambulance.

Then there was me. Helpless little me.

I had my growth spurt in sixth grade. It lasted exactly three months. I got my period, grew four inches, and stopped. I will forever be exactly five feet tall. I'm a gymnast chick. I'm tiny. Those girls with no boobs you see on TV, who stand on the balance beam during the Olympics and their knees and elbows look like they're bending the wrong way? That's me.

Most of the girls on my gymnastics team will get too tall or too fat or too bored to keep training. Not me. I'm the perfect size and shape. I've got NCAA Division I lines. And the scouts are interested.

On that day back in eighth grade, feeling helpless, watching them wheel Mary Alice down the hallway to the ambulance, I made a list in my head of things I needed to do that day. When I got back to class, I wrote them down:

1. Send Mary Alice a get-well card. Or balloons. Or something.
2. Run through floor routine again tonight after practice.
3. Call Mom, tell her I'll be late because I'm working the floor routine.
4. Make sure red competition leotard is clean.

The list made me feel like I was doing something, like life wasn't happening around me, or to me. The list made me feel like I was in charge of something in those moments after Mary Alice went to the hospital.

It made me feel not so small.

We lost the meet that weekend in March, but a high school coach from across town saw me compete. Afterward he came up and handed my dad his card.

"Your girl is Division One material, Dad." When the coach smiled, he had a dimple on one side of his face. "Guy Stevens. Give me a call next week. I'm at Westport High. Best public school athletics department in the Northwest. Our girls have taken the Class 4A championship at state the last three years."

My Dad thanked him, and then the coach turned to me.

"You got killer moves, little lady. If you can convince your dad to send you my way, we'll get you in shape for the Olympics." Later that summer, Coach Stevens invited us to a cookout. "My niece will be there," he said. "She's Beth's age and she'll be playing volleyball at Westport this fall."

And that's how I met Leslie Gatlin.

She wasn't as petite as I was, but I remember taking one look and thinking how delicate she looked. And tan. She seemed to be spun out of brown sugar and air, like a heavy rain might wash her away completely. Her dad was an asshole who talked about housing prices and market values without anyone else getting a word in edgewise. Her mom was slurring good-byes when they left that night, plastered on white wine spritzers.

Leslie and I talked about school at first—where she'd gone, where I'd gone—and at some point during that evening, my dad decided that I could change districts and go to Westport to train with Leslie's uncle. For some reason, I told Leslie about Mary Alice and about the list I made and how the list made me feel powerful and unafraid even in the midst of chaos.

Then we laughed and made a list together. It was a list of silly things that we would never do in high school:

1. Run when we weren't in a practice or competition.
   (It makes you look like you're not in control.)
2. Let any boy get to second base on the first date.
   (It makes you look desperate.)
3. Miss a game, a meet, or a practice for any reason.
   (It makes you look lazy.)
4. Drink booze before we were twenty-one.
   (It makes you look like a loser.)

We were in the driveway, lying on the hood of her dad's truck, staring up at the stars. The metal was still warm from baking in the summer sun all day. I asked Leslie how she'd gotten so tan, and she explained that she'd come back from vacation the day before. She told me all about her trip to Cape Cod and the sand and the sun and the sailing.

And a boy named Jake.

Thinking of that night made me cry again, this time harder. My head hurt so badly from the snot and the tears and the pressure that I could barely see.

I pulled up to the rear entrance of the school so I could go in the back door between the gym and the music building. The traffic out front seemed a little crazy and I knew I'd have a better shot of making it to the bathroom to wash my face and put on some mascara without being seen if I went in the back way.

I parked and grabbed my bag and blew my nose one last time. For some unknown reason the sky was clear and cloudless, and the sun was a little blinding for Seattle in the spring. Grateful for the excuse, I kept my sunglasses on and pulled the hood of my sweatshirt up.

I grasped the handle of the heavy back door and prepared to give it the big heave-ho muscle required to open it, but it was surprisingly light to my touch, and I realized too late that someone had hit the crash bar on the inside as I'd taken the handle. The door flew open like it was propelled by an explosive, and Bradley Wyst almost flattened me. He was moving so fast that he knocked my bag out of my hand and my sunglasses went clattering across the concrete.

"Dude! Look where the hell you're go—" He stopped short when he saw it was me. I stopped and picked up my sunglasses and put them back on without dusting them off, hoping he hadn't seen my eyes.

"Jesus, Beth."

"What, Brad?" I stared straight at him, daring him to say a word. It's a trick I learned with my little brother.

He seemed to be panting. He must've run the whole length of the building, from the senior parking lot to the back door. Brad was Jake's best friend from kindergarten and had been Macie's boyfriend since freshman year. He was taller than the rest of us, and usually quieter, the strong, silent type who stood at Macie's elbow during parties, smiling and refilling drinks, happy to let her do the talking. It was strange seeing him in a hurry.

Brad scooped up my bag and handed it to me. "Sorry. Where's Jillian?"

"Jillian?" I asked. "Macie should know. Isn't Macie here already?"

He made a sound that wasn't quite a snort and rolled his eyes. "Oh, Macie's here all right. Have you seen Jills?"

I shook my head, but he'd already run into the parking lot.

"If you see her, tell her to text me," he called over his shoulder.

I adjusted my hood again, then took a deep breath and heaved open the back door, hoping that I could make it through the morning crush to the bathroom without having to throw any elbows.

The back hall was deserted.

I stood at the door confused, fumbling to find my phone

and check the time. It said 8:20. We had ten minutes until the bell rang for first period.

Where the hell is everybody?

I went into a stall and locked the door behind me. I needed to think for a second—to figure out what I was going to say to Macie. How was I going to keep her from telling everyone that it was my fault? Somewhere buried in those Facebook posts on Leslie's wall, she must've seen the note. When she'd walked out of the bathroom this morning, she hadn't told anyone else to go to Leslie's page and post, only me.

That wasn't a mistake. There are no mistakes with Macie.

The door to the bathroom swung open, and through the narrow space between the stall partitions, I saw two junior girls come in; one of them was crying.

"I . . . just can't believe . . . she's . . . dead," she choked out.

The other one said nothing. She nodded and hugged her friend. I recognized them from the volleyball team.

"I mean . . . how can Macie stand out there and talk to them like she was her best friend?"

"Macie Merrick is a psycho, and she owns Katherine, Jillian, and Beth. You better not let any of them hear you talking like this unless you want to be next in the crosshairs."

I felt an explosion in the pit of my stomach. The heat raced into my throat and I turned just in time to hit the toilet and keep from throwing up on my bag.

The sound startled the girls at the sink.

The one who wasn't crying walked over and gently knocked on the stall door.

"Are you okay in there?"

"Fine," I said. "Ate something weird last night."

I flushed the toilet and unlatched the door. When they saw me, they froze. I fixed both of them with the stare that had silenced Brad earlier, then crossed to the sinks and cranked a large sheet of paper towel out of the dispenser. I turned on the cold water and gulped several mouthfuls straight from the tap before splashing some across my face with my hands.

I turned off the water, tore the paper towel from the dispenser, dried my face, then walked back to the stall for my bag. I returned to the mirror digging out some moisturizer and mascara. Both of the girls had their eyes trained on me when I looked up, and then quickly looked away.

"I overheard you say that Macie was talking to somebody?" I asked them, studying my reflection, then fishing for eyeliner. "Who was she talking to?"

The redhead frowned. "Um . . . the reporters? Out front? How'd you miss her when you walked in?"

Another day, I might have answered her. I might have asked her name. I might have told her that I came in the back door.

But on this day, I was already in the hallway with my bag.

Running.

4. JAKE

I hate treadmills. Boring as hell. I want to be headed somewhere when I run.

Running before school in Seattle is tricky. During the winter it's cold and in the spring I'm drenched, but I'm not afraid of a little water, and once you get going, you warm up pretty quick.

Besides, when I don't run, I can feel it.

I could feel it when I was sitting in class and couldn't concentrate enough to take notes. I could feel it when I saw Leslie in the hallway and she ignored me. I could feel it when Brad let loose with some crack and Coach made the whole team stay for an extra scrimmage.

When I run, none of that crap gets to me.

The farther I run, the smaller my problems get.

I know it's all about the chemicals in my brain and the way

my body deals with stress, but it seems way simpler than that. When I wake up and run, something shifts. And I don't mean the things in my life magically get better. Or even change.

It's more like I change.

It's not a big change. It's a tiny shift—like when my mom moves a picture frame a couple of inches to the right so that it's hanging level on the wall again. Before she does that, it's like all you can see in the whole living room—that crooked picture. Once it's fixed, all you notice is the picture. You don't spend time thinking about how screwed up it looks—just who's inside the frame.

Running is like that. It makes me see all the same stuff—really see it—without thinking about how screwed up it is.

This morning was warmer than it had been, and when the alarm went off at six a.m., I rolled out and pulled on the shorts and long-sleeve running shirt I had set out last night after I got back from Leslie's. I grabbed my Nano and headed downstairs to pull on my shoes by the front door.

As I passed Jillian's door, I heard something and stopped. The door to the media room was cracked open a bit and I could see a light in the corner. It was coming from the laptop Jillian and I share. My eyes were full of sleep crap, so I rubbed them and finally focused on Beth on the air mattress in the corner, peering at the screen. Her shoulders were shaking. The sound I'd heard was her sniffing.

I thought about asking her if she was okay, but Krista was

passed out next to her and Katherine was on the pull-out. Besides, Beth is always okay—or isn't interested in talking about if she isn't okay.

The sun was already coming up when I hit the sidewalk outside our house and started down the block. I love mornings like this in Seattle—you can see Mount Hood from the hill where we live, and when it's clear and the sun starts coming up, you get this awesome view that reminds you why it's not so bad to put up with the rain the rest of the time. The air was fresh and I thought about Leslie and wondered what time she'd made it to Portland last night.

I'd begged her to let me come.

"It'll just be easier if you're not involved," she said.

"But I am involved," I said.

She sighed and looked down at the floor. I hooked a finger under her chin and gently pulled it up toward my face. One more time I leaned in close to her. One more time I tried to kiss her. One more time she pulled away.

"Jake, don't."

I stepped back and shook my head. "I don't get you."

"I know," she said.

"What's wrong with me?"

"Nothing, Jake. Everything is right with you."

"Then why won't you kiss me?"

She didn't have an answer. She never did.

• • •

Thinking about Leslie crying late last night made me push my speed so I could get back home to shoot her a text. Mile six was a killer, but I punched through it and was walking the last block to cool down when Macie rounded the corner in her black 5 Series Bimmer, trying to break the sound barrier. If I hadn't been paying attention, I'd have stepped off the curb and been run over, but I stopped short as she blasted past me. She threw up a hand and smiled like she was on the campaign trail with her dad.

I shook my head and frowned, stepping into the street as she passed, then standing with my arms outstretched in her rearview mirror, silently asking, "What the hell?"

I'm sure she didn't see me. Macie Merrick never looks back.

No text from Leslie when I got back to my room. I shot her a message and jumped in the shower. No text when I got outta the shower, so I called her phone. No answer, so I left her a voice mail.

I was in the kitchen eating some cereal when my phone rang. I grabbed it and answered before I saw the ID. I knew it was her.

"Hey, dude." I smiled into the phone. "How's Portland?"

There was a pause on the other end. "Jake?"

It was Brad.

"Oh—hey, man. What's up? Sorry—thought you were Leslie."

There was a longer pause this time. "Oh. Shit."

"Brad?"

"You don't know yet?"

"Don't know what?"

"The girls were at your place last night, right?"

"Yeah," I said. "What don't I know?"

"You haven't . . . talked to them this morning?"

"I just got back from my run. Your girlfriend almost mowed me down on the corner, but no, I haven't talked to them."

"Oh, man."

Silence.

"Brad? Where are you? What is going on?"

"I'm at school." He paused. "Sitting here in my truck . . ." His voice trailed off.

I looked at the clock. What was he doing at school already? I felt a weird, tense place in my stomach.

"What don't I know, Brad?" My heart was racing again like I was still running. He was making me nervous.

"Hurry up and get here, and I'll— "

"Brad! Fucking tell me already."

Another long pause. I turned around and flipped on the water to rinse my bowl out.

"Leslie is dead," he said quietly.

I stood there, blinking, holding the phone in one hand and my cereal bowl in the other. The sound of the water against the stainless sink roared in my ears. I couldn't swallow.

I couldn't hear. Finally I gasped—a long, slow choke of air rattled into my chest and out again as soon as it came.

"What?"

It was all I could get out. I heard glass breaking. I saw my cereal bowl against the granite countertop. It had been circular and now it was tiny triangles—specks of white.

"They found her in her garage this morning—in her mom's car. It had been running all night."

"What do you mean?" I could hear the words he was saying, and they seemed to be coming out in order, but none of them made sense.

"She had a bag on her lap—like she was packed for a trip or something. But she never left the garage."

I tried to pick up the triangle of bowl on the counter but my hand wouldn't work, and as the shard fell into the sink with the others, I felt my knees begin to buckle. I leaned back against the counter as my mom rounded the corner with her briefcase, her heels clicking on the dark wood.

"Jake?" She said my name like a question. Her wide, blue eyes searched mine for answers, then darted to the shards of bowl on the counter and in the sink, the water running hard and loud as I slowly melted down the cabinets and onto the floor. I was holding on to my phone like it was the only thing that would keep me upright. As I looked at my mom—framed by the doorway—the room seemed to shift an inch or two, like the whole world had dropped off center to the left.

Not a big change.

But it was all I could see.

Brad kept saying my name into the phone. His voice sounded far away behind the roar in my ears. My face was hot and wet with sweat and something else. I couldn't see clearly and wiped at my eyes. My hand came away wet, and that's when I knew that I was crying. I felt a weight in my chest like I was underwater, and realized I needed to breathe—it wasn't happening by itself. I gasped and choked into the phone.

"Brad." And then again, louder. "*Brad.*"

"Yeah, man. I'm here."

"Where's Jillian?"

5. JILLIAN

I was pulling into the back parking lot when I saw Brad sprinting toward me; his long, lean frame didn't pause until he was sitting in my passenger seat.

"Drive," he said.

"What?"

"Starbucks. Now."

"Brad, we have like eight minutes until first period starts."

"No first period today—Jenkins is calling an assembly as soon as the reporters clear out."

I stepped on the gas.

I had seen the satellite dishes on the cluster of vans when I'd arrived this morning, and even though I was a thousand feet away on the next corner, I knew that Macie was standing in the epicenter, holding court. The only thing more spot-on than her fashion sense is her acumen for media relations.

She comes by it honestly.

When we were in kindergarten, her dad ran for city council. In fourth grade he was elected mayor. In eighth grade the good people of Seattle sent him to the state legislature. He was gunning for D.C. next, and if his movie star looks and silver tongue were any indication, he'd be there before we finished college. It's weird—he's got this magnetic pull. When he talks to you, you feel like you're the only person in the room, even though you're never the only person in the room. It's always a mob scene when he's around—even when it's just his family.

Macie has four brothers—two older, two younger. Mikey, Matty, Manny, and Marty. (Yeah, I know. Who does that to their kids?) They're not Mormons or anything. I don't even think Macie's mom and dad even particularly wanted a big family. Truth be told, they couldn't keep their hands off each other. They still can't.

Macie is definitely Daddy's girl.

"She's our rose among the thorns," her dad always says, beaming, when he's introducing the family on election night, after he declares victory. Her brothers look like a boy band—Mikey is the jock, Matty is the adorkable nerd, Manny is the skinny emo boy with the long bangs, and Marty is . . . well, the disaster. He's been smoking pot since he was ten, and the rumors about his drug use almost took down Mr. Merrick's campaign for state senate.

Watching him pull that one out of the fire was surreal. There was an ad that ran almost every commercial break during the local and national newscasts on the Big Three networks. It was a steady shot that had Mr. Merrick staring directly into the camera, eyes welling up but not shedding a single tear. This was righteous rage. This was the iron hand of justified anger. Macie and I stood right behind the camera and watched him in take after take as he leveled his gaze and squared his jaw and said, "The slander must stop. I'll stand up for you, like I stand up for my son. Let's circle the wagons and clean up Olympia."

It was after our first day of eighth grade—I'll never forget it: We were standing behind the camera guy while we watched the director and the campaign manager fight it out. Even though we were off to one side and in the corner, Macie was right in the middle of it. Her eyes were almost as bright as her father's are when a key light hits them. She couldn't get enough. She was quiet as her dad drove us home from the set. Everybody was quiet. No one was sure if the commercial would work, and if he didn't win this race, it'd be at least two years before Mr. Merrick could run for anything again.

We were pulling into her driveway when Macie broke the silence.

"Jillian and I are running for student council at Westport next year."

It was so matter-of-fact, so confident—but more than confident. It was shrewd, like she had a secret. I looked at her, then glanced up at her dad's reflection in the rearview mirror.

A movie star smiled back with eyes that welled up but didn't shed a single tear.

Everybody thinks it was that commercial that saved his race for state senate, but they forget that after our first day of eighth grade, Mr. Merrick went after it like he'd never campaigned before. He stood on cars at dealerships, cut ribbons at grocery stores, served food to the homeless, and attended four fund-raising dinners one Friday night and was up at five a.m. cooking pancakes at a Catholic church the next morning.

He was everywhere.

No one remembers that Marty disappeared to "stay with relatives" in Nevada somewhere for the whole month of October. They remember only that Mike Merrick was on every newscast for a month straight. They sort of cock their collective head to one side and barely remember the commercial if you mention it, but I know that the fire behind Mr. Merrick's fight that fall wasn't the ad at all.

It was that moment in the driveway when Macie went into the family business.

The Starbucks across the street from the school was almost empty when we pulled up. I parked way back on the side so nobody would see us. Brad ordered while I sat slumped in a leather club chair, staring out the front door and across the street at the ring of news vans. Piano jazz tinkled into my ears and the rhythm matched the syncopated sickness in my stomach. I jumped when my phone did—a text from Jake: `Where are you?`

This was ridiculous. I couldn't avoid him forever.

I swallowed as I tapped a finger onto the screen so that I could reply, but then Brad set down my Venti skinny vanilla latte and started pouring raw-sugar packs into his Grande drip.

"You okay?" he asked quietly.

I held the phone out so he could see the text from my brother.

"I can't run from him all day, Brad. He sleeps down the hall."

"But you don't have to see him before I do."

Brad and Jake have been best friends since kindergarten. Since the summer they started playing football together in the park down the street. Since girls had cooties.

"Lemme take this one, Jills."

I put down the phone and picked up my latte. It was sweet, and warm on my lips. As I sipped it, I stared into Brad's brown eyes. He was always so sure that nothing was really wrong, so confident that it could be "handled." He was the cool, collected pragmatist to Jake's headstrong hothead.

Katherine had summed it up best one night last summer:

"That boy don't care if the cat is black or white as long as it catches mice."

I smiled as I thought of it. Brad caught me and grinned back. "Atta girl," he said, wiping some foam off my upper lip with his fingertip. He popped it into his mouth and raised his eyebrows at me when he licked it off.

"So what's the plan?" I asked.

He grabbed my hand and helped me up.

"Thought you'd never ask," he said.

6. KATHERINE

As I stood next to Macie in front of the cameras and watched her taking questions from the reporters, all I could think about was Aunt Liza telling me that I didn't have to prove I was pretty. Before every pageant I'd ever competed in, Aunt Liza did my hair. Nobody could get a French twist quite as tight as she could, and we always talked while she worked with the brushes and the pins. I always asked if she was coming, and every time I asked, she said the same thing:

"Sweet pea, I know you got more brains and more talent than the rest of them girls combined, and I've never even seen 'em. You ain't got to prove you're pretty to me."

Macie had come to prove something this morning. She was dressed for a funeral. Her outfit was perfect and professional—and all black. Her lips were red like blood, and when Principal Jenkins had seen her *click click click* out onto the front steps of the school, he'd looked relieved. The reporters saw a Merrick and rushed on over to us like Jenkins was yesterday's tuna fish.

Macie made the local evening news last year when we ran for student council and won. We were the first two females ever to win the president and vice president positions at Westport High, and she'd made the most of it—kept my hand up in the air for so long clutched in hers when the reporters showed up for the vote announcement that my whole arm fell asleep.

I remember standing there and asking through my smile why there were reporters in the gym.

"Because I had my dad's press secretary tip off her contacts, silly," she hissed. "Keep smiling. This is gonna get you into Harvard Law."

So I smiled. Hard. Till it hurt.

Today, I didn't have to ask Macie how the reporters knew about a suicide at a local high school. I knew. She'd probably sent two or three text messages and an email from her phone at Jillian's this morning. She'd known exactly what time she and I should walk out onto the front steps.

"Miss Merrick, as student body president, what's the message you have for your fellow students today?" It was Mary Jackson from Channel 13 News.

"That suicide is not the answer," said Macie in a clear, concerned voice. She looked stricken. "High school can be hard. The schedule is demanding. The social stress is high.

But there is always another answer," she said. "Our message today at Westport, and at high schools all over our city, should be that there is always hope."

"Did you know Leslie Gatlin?" asked Hank Arnold from Action News 5.

"I did know her, Hank, though we weren't close. On behalf of the student body here at Westport, I want to send our deepest sympathies and condolences to her family. I can't imagine what her parents must be feeling this morning."

Had to hand it to Macie. She was good at this. It was like watching a pro running back dodging linemen all the way to the end zone.

I glanced over at Brad, who was standing behind the cameras across from Macie, but he was looking down at his phone, and before I could catch his eye, he took several steps backward and answered a call. I heard him whisper, "Hey, Jillian," but I couldn't hear anything else.

"Did Leslie seem agitated or sad the last time you spoke?" Hank followed up with Macie.

"I wouldn't want to speculate on Leslie's mental health," said Macie, then she looked directly into the camera. "I hadn't spoken to her in several weeks. I just . . ." And there was a pause so slight that if you were watchin' her at home, you might not have caught it unless you were staring right at her. Her lip quivered and for a hot second her eyes got a little glossy, like a pat of butter melting on a pancake. Almost tears—but not quite. "I can't imagine what must have been going on in her mind." Macie swallowed hard and blinked several times, obviously shaken. "What kind of anguish does one have to be in to devastate the people you leave behind?"

Out of the corner of my eye, I saw Brad take off running toward the senior parking lot, as Mary Jackson jostled for position in front of Macie and asked, "Macie, to your knowledge, was Leslie bullied?"

"Thank you for asking, Mary." Macie was all business now. "Principal Jenkins has instituted a zero-tolerance policy for bullying. One of our major initiatives this year on the student council has been to institute a campus-wide bully-free zone. I've already talked this morning to Katherine Fraisure, my stuco vice president, and my boyfriend, Brad Wyst, the captain of the football team. We're planning to head up a committee to make counseling services and peer support groups available here at Westport."

As the questions continued, Macie deferred a couple to Principal Jenkins, who joined us on the front steps, and I slowly lowered my eyes and glanced at my watch. Ten minutes until the assembly. I barely had enough time to sneak over to Starbucks for some tea and a Perfect Oatmeal. The idea of sitting through an assembly on an empty stomach was enough to kill me. Deep down, though, beneath the hunger, there was a knot growing in my stomach that had been there since I'd woken up and heard Beth crying this morning. It was fear, plain and simple, and the more Macie talked, the worse it felt.

I had a bad feeling about all this. Leslie had been bullied. I knew. Macie knew it. We knew, because we'd done the bullying. Macie could spin it all she wanted, but at the end of the day, now there was tape of her lying about what went on.

I stepped back as Macie crowded forward toward the rush of mics. *If you think I'm going down with this ship, you don't know me very well.*

As I slowly stepped to the side of Principal Jenkins and down the stairs toward my car in the senior lot, I saw Beth standing in the doorway of the lobby, in front of the trophy cases, her mouth flung so far open, I was afraid she might swallow a fly. Her wispy blond pixie cut was freshly parted, and the freckles on her nose stood out against her fair skin. She was even paler than usual.

I stepped out of the shot and around the bank of cameras, then slipped in the door.

"Beth?"

"Katherine, what is she saying?"

I glanced back out at the mob scene on the front steps. "Oh, you know Macie. She's makin' it up as she goes along."

Beth's eyes didn't move an inch from the back of Macie's head.

"No, Katherine. What is she saying about me?"

When I put my hand on her shoulder, I could feel her shaking through her hoodie.

"Beth, honey, she's not sayin' a damn thing about you. She's just talking about safe zones and antibullying intiatives."

Beth turned and looked at me. Her eyes were red and puffy. She had moisturizer under her nose that wasn't rubbed in, and her eyeliner was a crooked mess. That girl can nail a double layout dismount with a half twist, but it's a good day when her socks match.

"Katherine," she whispered, her lips trembling. "You have to help me."

"Are you okay?" I asked.

Beth pulled me through the hall, toward the doors that led to the back parking lot. The benches outside were deserted. Everyone was around front for the media feeding frenzy. She pulled me down onto a bench by the door and started to sob.

"This is all my fault, Katherine. I was the meanest one to Leslie. Macie's gonna tell everyone that I'm the one to blame."

"What are you talking about?"

"You're the only one who can help me. You're the only one who has ever shown even a spark of standing up to Macie."

"Help you with what, Beth?"

She was crying so hard she couldn't say.

I held her for a while until her tears subsided, then I sat her up and wiped my finger under her nose to smooth in her face cream.

"I'm going to get some tea at Starbucks. You comin'? Macie can handle this."

Beth shook her head. "No, I can't leave. I have to hear what she says."

I nodded. "I'll meet you in the assembly with a chamomile. Sound good?"

She smiled, and I picked up my purse.

When I pulled up to the Starbucks across the street, I saw Jillian holding her phone up to Brad at a table inside. And I don't know if it was the way she looked at him, or the way he brushed that speck of foam off her lip, or the way he grabbed her hand as they stood up to leave, but something in me got real quiet and I had a feeling something was up.

Brad held the door for Jillian, and I watched them turn away from my car as they walked down the side of the building to Jillian's car and got in it. Then Brad talked while Jillian sipped coffee and rubbed her temples with her hands. And just when I thought Jills was gonna turn the key in the ignition, Brad reached over and took her hand off the steering wheel and kissed it, real soft.

It felt like time stood still—like I was watching something I shouldn't be, like in sixth grade when I found the Christmas presents too early and kept sneaking down to Mama's room to look at the boxes under the bed when Aunt Liza took a nap. It felt all wrong, but I couldn't stop looking.

As I sat there watching, slouched down in my seat like a bandit, Brad took Jillian's face in his hands and leaned in and kissed her. Not a peck; a long, slow, strong kiss that made me gasp out loud like a damn fool. And they sat there kissing for a good long time, at least a minute or two.

Long enough for me to gather my senses, grab my phone, and take three pictures.

I wasn't sure why I took them.

But all at once, I had a plan.

7. BETH

When Jenkins started the assembly, it was silent, and that's saying something. Over one thousand living, breathing anythings are generally noisy. Over one thousand high schoolers can be deafening. I've heard it. Last fall when I scored a perfect 10 on the beam in competition, I thought the roof was falling into the gym, the cheering was so loud. Coach Stevens was the only one who was quiet. He stood there looking at me as I walked toward him, his hands on his hips, shaking his head. It wasn't until I got right up to him that I saw he was crying.

He waited until I got next to him, then he grabbed me and wrapped me up in the biggest bear hug I've ever had and whispered into my neck so softly:

"Atta girl. You're going all the way."

That made me choke up, and of course, I had to stare up into the lights to keep my eyeliner from running all over the place, and I just hate watching wimpy girls cry—especially at the Olympics. I mean, I am all for being happy that you win and jumping up and down and everything, but, c'mon. Crying and whispering "Thank you, God" to the ceiling? Because God wanted you to get a perfect 10 on the beam that day? Like he didn't have anything to look after in Haiti? Quake victims have no clean water, and half the kids on the island are dying of dysentery, but, sure—God stopped by the gym at Westport High in Seattle to make sure that you nailed the dismount.

Urrrgh. I just hate that.

And I hate peppermint tea, which is what Katherine brought back when she slipped into the assembly and slid into our bleacher.

"Sorry," she whispered. "They were all out of the chamomile. Hope peppermint is okay."

Peppermint is not okay. It makes me think of Christmas at Grandma Cratchin's, which is always awful and long and boring, and Grandpa always makes us take turns reading Luke 2 in the living room before we can open presents, while Grandma is pouring everybody enough peppermint tea to make us float to Bethlehem without boats.

But I just took the cup and smiled back at her. There's nothing to do but smile back at Katherine's smile. It's a billion watts of perfect teeth that's been practiced in front of a mirror for enough hours to win tiaras and sashes in seven different pageant systems so far. It's sort of a weapon of mass destruction, really. Not a lot of black girls winning pageants in Seattle—or seats on the student council at Westport High until last year.

It's wild. Macie replaced Jillian on the ticket without even telling her. Just showed up, and blam—Katherine was the VP. It was nuts that first week of school last fall. Jillian was crazed, trying to keep up with what was going on, but not stepping on Macie's toes. Trying not to let the news that she was high pissed show on her face.

But make no mistake. She was pissed. Pissed, but silent. The Jillian way.

Everybody was silent now, as Principal Jenkins ticked off the facts:

1. FACT: Leslie Gatlin was found dead this morning of carbon monoxide poisoning in her mother's Audi, which had been idling for some seven hours with the garage door closed.
2. FACT: Leslie Gatlin's mother had called the paramedics, who had rushed to the scene.
3. FACT: After trying to resuscitate Leslie Gatlin, she was pronounced dead on arrival at University of Washington Medical Center.
4. FACT: Students were asked to seek the help of the guidance counselor, Marilynne Hennesy, if they needed to talk with someone about any feelings that Leslie's death was bringing up for them, or any suicidal

thoughts they might be having as a result.

5. FACT: Student council president Macie Merrick had a few words to say before we were dismissed.
6. FACT: Students were asked to report to regularly scheduled classes beginning with second period at the end of this assembly.

When Jenkins mentioned Macie's name, she slid from her seat on our bleacher near the front, took the cup of tea out of Katherine's hand, swallowed a quick sip, handed it back without looking at any of us, and strode toward the waiting mic in Jenkins's outstretched hand.

"I don't know what to think about this . . . loss." Her voice was low but strong. "I don't know what to think about anything, but I do know how I feel about this. I feel angry. I feel robbed. I feel cheated of knowing our friend. I may not know what to *think* about this loss, but I sure know what I want to *do* about this loss."

The gym was silent. There were people sniffing. Looking down. I saw the volleyball girls from the bathroom clasp hands; the redhead had tears running down her cheeks.

"I've spoken with Principal Jenkins this morning, and we are going to hold a suicide-awareness seminar during lunch hours on Thursday. This afternoon at the student council meeting I will be bringing a proposal to set up a memorial scholarship fund in Leslie Gatlin's name for a senior who enters college specifically to pursue the mental health fields, so that her parents can always remember with heads held high the impact that Leslie had here at our school; that because she lost her life, other lives will be saved.

"And finally, we will begin talks to institute class credit for shifts at the TeenReach Hotline—Seattle's teen suicide prevention line—to make sure that there is an ear for every student in need at this school, freshman or senior, black or white, boy or girl, gay or straight."

Macie grew silent again and slowly surveyed the assembly before looking down at the mic in her hands for a moment. "Maybe you're like me, and you don't know what to think of all this. Well, today I want you to feel with me," she said, banging a clasped fist against her chest, her voice rising. "And then tomorrow I want you to come back to this school and I want you to *do* with me. I want you to help me do things to make sure that this will not happen again. Not on our watch. Not at our school. Not at Westport. Never again!"

Over a thousand teenagers roared in the way that only a thousand teenagers can. It sounded again like the roof might fall into the gymnasium.

I realized that Katherine wasn't sitting beside me anymore. She had slipped away somewhere. But off at the far end of the gym, by the doors that led to the athletic offices, I caught a glimpse of Coach Stevens. He was silent, standing there as I walked toward him.

I stood in front of him for what seemed like forever.

"Beth?" he said. Only it was a question. And in that question, everything I was afraid of came blazing to the surface. Coach Stevens reached out his arms to hug me. "I know you loved my niece," he said, so softly I thought for a moment that I'd imagined it.

Slowly, I looked back over my shoulder. Macie, Brad, and Jillian were standing in the circle painted in the center of the gym, watching me.

I turned back to Coach Stevens, frozen, my mind racing. He just stood there with his arms out—an invitation, really. I wanted to run into them, to hug him, to tell him the whole story, to let him know that it would be okay. To cry onto his warm-up jacket until the tears ran out.

Instead, I turned toward the exit in the corner by his office, and for the second time that day, I ran.

8. JAKE

When Jillian and I were little, before we could speak words you'd recognize, we spoke our own language. Dad told me about it one time when we were painting the new cabinets he'd put up in the garage.

"What would we say?" I asked him.

"Who knows?" he said with a chuckle. "But you were definitely communicating. The two of you would laugh and sing and jabber and talk yourselves to sleep. Sometimes it would take hours. But you never cried. You were happy as clams just being with each other."

Dad paused while he poured paint from a five-gallon bucket into a roller tray. He put down the bucket and turned to wipe his hands on a rag, and glanced out toward the street.

"So funny . . . ," he said softly. "Best one ever. Best moment of my life," he said, smiling. "Your mom and I leaning over the counter with a cheap bottle of red, eating take-out stir fry, and listening to you and your sister giggling over that little baby monitor walkie-talkie. We would never have planned on twins. Sometimes life gives you what you need, not what you think you want."

I caught a drip with the brush before it rolled off the cabinet door. "I wonder what we were saying?"

"Dunno," he said, dipping a brush into the paint and edging out some inside shelves. "I always told your mom that you were giving Jillian NFL stats, but secretly I liked to think that you were telling her that you had her back—that everything was going to be okay."

Today everything is not okay. Today nothing feels like it will ever be right again.

Mom called her assistant when she found me in the kitchen, and told him to clear her schedule for the morning. She kicked off her shoes and sat down on the rug at the kitchen sink and just held me for a minute. It felt so weird. I've been taller than she is since I was in eighth grade, but I just sat there and cried into her shoulder.

Then she got up and made me some hot chocolate. She didn't ask me any questions. She didn't tell me what to do. She just sat there with me. She listened when I talked. She was quiet when I didn't.

Finally, I told her I had to go to school. I told her I had to find Jillian. She didn't try to make me stay home. She didn't say that it would be okay. She didn't say anything at all except "I love you." Then she dashed off a note to Principal Jenkins and slipped it to me along with a kiss as I walked out the door.

It was almost noon when I got in my car, and I had four texts from Brad asking where I was. I texted him *on my way* and drove to school.

Lunch was in full swing when I showed up. I checked in at the office and dropped off the note that Mom had written me, then headed to my locker. When I walked up to it, Brad saw me and was at my elbow almost immediately, as I watched Jillian, Macie, Krista, and Katherine head down the stairs to lunch in the cafeteria.

"Hey," he said. "C'mon, let's get some food."

"I'm not hungry," I said, following Brad toward the stairs where the girls had disappeared.

"Hold up, man," Brad said. "Are you okay?"

"No," I said, suddenly angry. "I'm not okay."

Brad held up both hands as we walked into the mayhem of the cafeteria. "I'm not the enemy," he said quietly. "And neither is Jillian."

"What's that supposed to mean?" I snapped, a little too loudly. A couple of girls at the table near the door turned around, and Brad pulled me over by the bank of vending machines. Macie had led a charge in the student council last fall to dump the Doritos and Cokes. Now the glass of the shiny new machines gleamed over Caesar salads and fruit juices.

"C'mon, Jake," Brad whispered. "Not here. I know you had a thing for Leslie, but it's not Jillian's fault that she's dead. Or Macie's, for that matter. It's Leslie's fault. Plain and simple."

I leveled my gaze at the table across the room. Macie had seen us and was glancing over at us every few seconds—watching us but pretending not to.

"Besides, Jake. She just wasn't that into you, man. She barely gave you the time of day for the last few months."

I looked at Brad. "You don't know what you're talking about," I said. "Jillian knows something about what happened last night. I'm guessing your girlfriend does, too. Leslie was supposed to go to her aunt's in Portland."

"How do you know?" Brad asked.

"Because I talked to her last night. She was supposed to call me when she got there. She never left her garage," I said. I took a deep breath. I could feel a choking feeling in the back of my throat.

Brad put a hand on my shoulder. "Jake, there's no way to explain this. It doesn't make sense, because killing yourself is . . . senseless. It's a crazy thing to do. Nothing about it is logical."

"And you know what's even less logical?" I asked. "Me leaving her house at eleven thirty last night with her set to drive to Portland, and Leslie being dead in her garage this morning.

What happened between the time I left and the moment she decided to sit in her garage and breathe car exhaust until she didn't wake up, Brad?"

"I don't know, man," Brad said.

"I'll bet you and Jillian and Macie do," I said.

"Now is not the time, Jake," Brad said, grabbing my arm as I headed toward their table by the windows.

I shook free of his grip on my arm. "It's as good a time as any."

9. JILLIAN

I knew that Jake was in the cafeteria before I saw Macie catch a glimpse of him, and then pretend that she hadn't. That's the thing about being a twin: Somehow you know. It's not magical; it's powerful. The difference being that magic doesn't exist, but power does.

Power exists for Macie in the way that she orchestrates the moments in her life. For Brad, the power is there in his kiss—in the moments when he feels like he's given Macie the slip. Between Jake and me there is this power of knowing—this real, deep knowing.

I knew the minute he fell in love with Leslie Gatlin that summer after eighth grade. He came back to the hotel suite. Mom and Dad were asleep in their room, and I had opened the sliding glass door off the balcony to listen to the surf pound the sand. I was standing there on the balcony in a hoodie and shorts when he walked into the room.

"Hey," I heard him say behind me, softly.

"Hey," I said without turning around. I could feel the moonlight reflecting off my cheeks. I licked my lips and tasted the salt in the air that had settled in the fine mist.

We were quiet for a while, listening to the swoosh-crash of the waves.

"Is Leslie a good kisser?" I asked without looking at him.

"Yeah," he said softly.

There was no protest or denial. He knew that I knew.

I glanced behind me and saw his big, goofy grin. His nose was a little red from sunburn, and it looked like he was blushing even though I knew he wasn't. Jake isn't that guy. He's never embarrassed of anything.

That's one of the main differences between us. I'm pretty much embarrassed about everything.

"What happened?" I asked.

"We were just walking down the beach," he said.

"Just?" I asked with a laugh. "You don't 'just' do anything, Jake."

He smiled and pulled my hood over my eyes.

"Hey!" I punched him lightly on the arm.

"Don't hurt your knuckles, Jills."

I shook my head and rolled my eyes. We stared at the water

some more, our elbows touching, side by side on the balcony rail. "Macie's gonna be really mad," I said.

"Macie's always mad about something," Jake said.

"She really likes you," I said.

"Macie Merrick likes herself," said Jake. "Lately she's liked the way she looks standing next to me. Trust me, she'll have a new crush on half the football team before the bell rings at the end of the first day. This is high school now."

"Yeah, but Macie isn't making this call," I said. "You are."

Jake was quiet for a moment. "I'm not making a call, Jills. I'm following one." He smiled, but not at me. He was looking out there, somewhere, to the tracks on the sand that ran together, the footprints all mixed up.

My stomach was all mixed up now, sitting at the lunch table watching Macie watch Jake getting closer and closer. She had this way of looking up through her dark lashes, mascara perfectly in place, eyes expertly lined. It was the look she got when she was about to pull out the big guns.

Krista was sitting directly across from me, and I saw her peer over my shoulder through her vintage glasses. "Look out," she said. "Incoming."

I didn't turn around until I heard him say my name.

"Jillian."

It wasn't exactly a question. It wasn't exactly an accusation.

I turned around and saw Brad standing at Jake's elbow. Jake's eyes were wet and bright, and his jaw was flexed. He was trying not to say more.

"Jake . . ." I jumped up and tried to hug him. He stepped back, waving me off.

"I need to talk to you," he said intently. "Alone."

"Oh, I don't think that'll be necessary, Jake." Macie said, batting her eyelashes. "We're all friends here. We don't mind."

Jake placed both hands on the table and leaned toward her, slowly. "We are not friends, Macie, and I don't give a shit what you mind and what you don't."

It was so fierce that everybody at three tables around ours went silent and turned their heads. Of course, when Macie has an audience, it's over. It's like saying "Sic 'em" to a pit bull, or "Amen" to a Baptist preacher.

Macie slowly pushed her tray back and slid her chair away from the table. She tugged the hem of her black skirt toward her knee, then crossed her legs so that her sheer black hose caught the light from the window overlooking the football field behind her. She leaned back with a sweet smile on her face and crossed her arms over her chest. Then, as if addressing a kindergartner, she spoke very slowly to my brother.

"Jake. You're obviously very upset. And Jillian isn't going anywhere with you while you're acting like a crazy person. So, I suggest that you say whatever it is that you have to say to her right now, right here, in front of me and Brad, and Katherine and Krista and Beth, and then we'll all be able to give you a hug, or hold a little prayer meeting, or whatever the hell it is you need to get your shit back together."

My heart raced. I realized that I was biting my tongue between my teeth. Hard. So hard it hurt. Jake was leaning over the table toward Macie, breathing like he'd just run a mile in five minutes.

"Macie, you are my best friend's girlfriend," he said slowly. "So I'm going to be kind about this. You hated Leslie because I liked her. She knew it and everybody else here did too. Since ninth grade, you've been an outright bitch to her, and now she's dead. I'm going to find out how you were involved in this. When I do, you are going down, and I'm taking your daddy down with you."

There were screams from the freshmen three tables away who were making the goalie of the JV soccer team drink a mixture of ketchup, milk, and beef Stroganoff. Apparently he'd lost a bet. There were bells ringing and announcements being made, but none of us could take our eyes off Macie. Her eyes narrowed at Jake as she slowly stood and leaned against the table toward him until they were nearly nose to nose.

"Let me recap the morning news for you, Jake. Leslie Gatlin committed suicide. Nobody pushed her in front of a bus. Nobody tied her up in that car and locked the garage door. She made a choice, Jake, and she didn't choose you."

Then Macie's eyes softened, and the tension dropped

out of her body. For the first time all day, she looked tired.

"Leslie made the wrong choice, Jake," she said softly. "Anybody with half a brain and one eye open would have chosen you."

Jake caught a breath and looked quickly out at the bleachers on the far side of the football field. He was blinking and pulling at his right eye. He was trying not to cry.

"C'mon, man. Let's walk it off." Brad grabbed Jake's elbow and propelled him toward the door.

I watched as they walked past the vending machines and back toward the stairs. Brad turned around and caught my eye as they left. He jerked his chin up just slightly and winked once, then he turned, tossed an arm around Jake, and headed up the stairs.

"*Whoooooo.*" Macie blew out a deep breath and ran a hand through her long hair. "Wow. That was intense."

For a moment, no one moved or spoke. Then Krista tossed back the last sip of Diet Coke in her can and sat forward with a bright smile. "Hi. I'm Krista Abernathy and you're watching Teen Suicide Week with Jake Walker on Lifetime. Television for Boring Women."

Macie laughed hard. Maybe too hard. Too hard for Beth's and Katherine's taste anyway.

"Jesus, Krista," whispered Beth.

"What?" Krista said in her typical monotone flatline. "Too soon?"

Macie was still laughing and now wiping tears from under her perfect eye makeup with a napkin. "Oh my God," she gasped.

Katherine stood up abruptly and began gathering her things.

"Oh, c'mon, everybody. Comedy equals tragedy plus time," Macie said.

Katherine looked at her. "It's been five hours, Macie. We need some more time."

Macie was incredulous. "Oh, puh-leeease." She rolled her eyes. "Don't everybody go getting all uptight on me now. This is exactly the time to start capitalizing on the silver lining here."

"Silver . . . lining?" Beth was frowning, confused.

I felt confused, too, but not for the same reason. Not for any reason I could put my finger on. I knew what was coming from Macie. She always had an angle. I knew her almost as well as I knew Jake.

"Oh, please. My Harvard application essay just wrote itself this morning. Yours did too, Katherine. And the extra-curriculars this is going to generate . . ." Her voice trailed off. "By the time the student council meeting ends today, we'll all be running a committee formed around teen suicide. Ladies, our college applications just moved to the top of the short-list pile."

"Look, I didn't like Gatlin any better than any of y'all did," Katherine said. "But—"

"You don't say." Macie cut her off with a short, incredulous laugh. "I think Leslie thought you were her best friend for the first few weeks last year."

Katherine's eyes flashed, and she hissed at Macie through clenched teeth. "I'm just saying a little sensitivity is in order here."

"I'll tell you what's in order, Katherine, is a PowerPoint of photos that we can use at Saturday's memorial service in the gym. As yearbook editor, I hope you'll be on top of that. Krista, I can only imagine the Photoshop work that is going to be required to make pictures of Leslie suitable for public consumption."

"I'm on it," Krista deadpanned. "There's this little thing called the Healing Brush. It does wonders for sun damage."

Katherine sighed heavily, picked up her tray and her bag, and wordlessly clicked across the cafeteria linoleum like it was a runway.

Macie smiled after her.

"What's her deal?" asked Krista.

"I don't know, exactly," said Macie.

She turned to me, and I felt my cheeks burn even though I willed them not to. "Put Katherine on suicide watch, will you, Jillian? Can't have my VP cooking her own goose before we get the call-center volunteer program off the ground."

10. KATHERINE

Krista Abernathy makes my skin crawl. 'Course, I'd never say that to her face or anything. Aunt Liza taught me early on that nice girls don't let on when they don't like somebody.

"It's part of keeping your cards close to your chest," she said. "If you can't find something nice to say about somebody, you just smile and say, 'Well, bless your heart.'"

It was hard to find something nice to say about Krista, in my opinion, so I generally just tried to say nothing to her at all. She was the first one I ever met—first one I ever laid eyes on at this sorry-ass school where I wound up junior year. She's one of those white girls who will not eat: skin and bones, constantly smoking cigarettes, and has these bangs cut just a little too short in a line straight across her forehead. She claims they make her look like Bettie Page. Personally, I think they make her look like Porky Pig's girlfriend from Looney Tunes.

Regardless, Macie thinks Krista looks cool and "retro." "Krista is a hot hipster chick," Macie says, giggling about her bright-red, cat's-eye glasses. "She found those at this supercool vintage store over in Capitol Hill. I love it. She's fierce."

Maybe she is. Maybe "hip" just isn't "pretty."

I'm not sure what Macie Merrick saw in Krista. Jillian tells me Krista's daddy dropped dead of a heart attack at the dinner table. Turned out the autopsy revealed he was on so much OxyContin that he'd blown a clot and had a stroke right there over a petite filet.

Krista generally looks bored and above it all and like she can't wait to have another cigarette, but she sure lit up the first time she saw me. Walked right up to me at the registration for new students the week before school started last year.

"Hi," she said, extending her hand. "I'm Krista."

"Katherine," I said, taking her hand and using my "evening gown portion of our competition" smile. "It's a pleasure."

Before I realized what was happening, she pulled me in close and whispered, "Thank God you're black. I was hoping we'd get some decent color this year."

"Excuse me?" I asked, smile frozen in place.

"I'm on the Welcome Committee for the student council," she said. "C'mon. Wait'll Macie gets a load of you."

And that was how it happened. Macie smiled with her mouth right away that night, but her eyes were holdin' back a secret. Maybe two. She or Krista was always at my elbow that night, and Mama smiled like a possum eatin' briars. "Look at you, Katherine. You've already made friends with the student council members. That's just fantastic. Oh, sweetheart, I just knew that you'd make friends right away."

I wanted to sass her. I wanted to say, "Mama, these girls are not my friends. These girls want to earn their race-relations badge." But I held my tongue and thought about Aunt Liza. *Don't show your cards, Li'l K.*

Macie showed me to the right table in the gymnasium, and Krista tagged along with me and Mama, who insisted I take the tour of the whole damn campus. Finally, I waved good-bye and walked toward my car. Mama had met me at the school after stopping by a regional Miss Teen USA preseason orientation to pick up entrance forms and meet some of the other local participants. As soon as it was final that we were moving, she'd called to make sure we were all squared away with contacts and residency requirements.

As I beeped the automatic locks on the silver BMW Daddy had gotten me for my sixteenth birthday, I heard a voice behind me.

"Wow. Is this your car?"

I jumped a little as I turned around and saw Macie standing with her arms crossed, leaning against a jet-black model of the same car I drove. I was quick to push my smile back up.

"Oh . . . hey, Macie," I said. "Didn't see you there."

Macie had a funny look on her pretty face. "Didn't expect you to drive something this . . ."

I let my smile go. "Nice?" I finished her sentence.

Macie just stared at me in silence—like she was sizing me up for a gown. Mama's stylist friend Darius, who always helps me pick out my evening gowns and swimsuits, uses the same look when he's peering at me, trying to imagine me in sequins or bugle beads or a sheer black organza.

After a moment, she cocked her chin to one side and smiled at me with just her mouth again. "Meet us at Marv's," she said.

"Us?" I asked. When she spoke she sounded almost weary. "Katherine," she said, "won't you please privilege me and several of my dearest friends with the honor of your presence this evening?"

She was making fun of me. At least I thought she was.

"Oh, Macie, that's so sweet of you. I think I'm just a little tired from the move this week and— "

"Katherine." Macie's voice stopped me. "Do I have to spell this out for you? We're the cool kids. You're the new girl. This is your invite."

"You don't even know me," I said.

"I know enough," she said. "Four-point-oh grade point average at Lithonia High School; daughter of Daysun Fraisure, lead litigator for Clarence, River, and DeKalb; first runner-up Miss

Atlanta Teen two years ago; winner Miss Georgia Teen last year."

My eyes were wide, and I laughed a little in spite of myself. "But . . . how did you . . . ?"

"There's an app for that," she said, holding up her phone. "You've got quite a web presence, you know."

I looked back at the school, then down at my watch.

"Come," she said. "I've got a proposition for you."

When I looked up, she was smiling at me again—this time with her eyes.

Krista and Beth were both in the booth already when I arrived at Marv's Diner with Macie.

"Here she is," Krista said. "Beth, Katherine. Katherine, Beth."

I shook Beth's hand. She looked up at me, and then over at Macie, and back at me. "Oh. My. God," she said quietly. "You're, like, twelve feet tall."

We all laughed. "No," I said. "I'm just wearing heels."

"What are you talking about?" Beth's eyes were wide, and she was shaking her head back and forth. "I already hate you. You're, like, twice as tall as me."

"And you're gorgeous and smart and poised and confident," said Macie. "My God, Katherine, now I hate you too." She held my gaze for a minute, then burst into laughter. Beth and Krista joined her. I stood there blinking, confused.

Macie saw my expression and smiled, wiping her eyes.

"Let me explain," she said. "I'm running for student council president this fall. I've been on the fence about my running mate. I decided tonight that you're it."

"Macie." I shook my head. "I'm going to be real busy with a couple of pageants to prepare for comin' right up. I have a real shot at Miss Teen USA this year, and I'm countin' on that scholarship money, so—"

"So you should do it," Krista said, interrupting me.

When I looked over at her, she was boring holes through those cat's-eye glasses, and that's the first time I felt it—the way she looked at me like I was a commodity, like I was the prize to be won. That was the first time she made my skin crawl.

Macie just smiled at me and patted the booth next to her. "Sit," she chirped. "Chat."

I gingerly slid into the booth next to Macie. The waiter came and took our orders. Krista got coffee, Beth asked for a salad, Macie ordered a Diet Coke with a lime.

"What are you having, Katherine?" she asked me.

When I hesitated, Krista cut in. "Second thoughts!" she said, then brayed like my granddaddy's donkey Moonshine did that night the skunk got into the barn when I was a little girl.

"I'm fine with water." I smiled at the waiter.

When he left, Macie turned to me. "Elections are two weeks away. Nominations are due by the end of the day on Monday. I've been class president since ninth grade. Jillian always runs as my VP, but this year, we can run for student council, and I don't want to risk running with her against the seniors. I've decided to make a change."

"Why?" I asked.

"Because if I'm going to win, I need the minority vote," she said.

My brow creased as I tried to put these pieces together. "And they'll vote for juniors like you and me because . . ."

"Because you've got the right heritage," Macie said.

Her words hit me like Mississippi humidity on a hot summer day. That was it. I was done here. I stood up. "Macie, I may be from the South, but I did not just bump off the turnip truck yesterday. Don't know who you think you're talkin' to, but I am not about to be—"

"The most popular girl in school on the first day?" Macie wasn't smiling. She arched an eyebrow, then took a deep breath and squeezed the lime into the Diet Coke the waiter set down on the table.

"Your call, Katherine," she said. "I'm not a racist. I just know how this works. My dad is a state senator. I know all about campaigning and I know even more about winning."

I stood there, unsure what my next move was.

"I know you're deeply offended," Macie said sharply, "which leaves only one question unanswered."

"What's that?" I asked, my smile frozen like the ice in Daddy's bourbon.

"Why are you still standing here?"

Krista and Beth were watching Macie like she was the best TV show they'd ever seen. I had to admit she was pretty sly. But she was no match for Aunt Liza, and that's who was on the playlist in my brain. *Don't you let some white gal take yo' power, Li'l K. You jump right in there and wrassle that gator to the ground. Ain't nobody else gonna do it for you.*

I brushed a wisp of hair out of my lipstick and sat down again. "I want a recommendation from your father to Columbia, Harvard, and Stanford whether we win or lose," I said.

"Atta girl," Macie said. "Done."

"And I won't be makin' any big speeches or stayin' after school till all hours to make posters for the prom or whatever fool thing your student council wants done next."

"Understood," Macie said. "I just need you there smiling and waving whenever there are newsworthy events."

"One more thing," I said. "Who do you know in the pageant system around here?"

"I think we can help you with that, too," Macie said slowly, and shot a look at Krista.

"No . . ." Krista looked delighted. "You wouldn't," she said. Beth looked down at her salad and pushed a tomato around.

Macie turned back to me with a grin so full of mischief that Aunt Liza woulda burst into spontaneous prayer over her right there on the spot. "There's a girl in our class whose mom just so happens to be a former beauty queen herself. She's in with every judge on the whole circuit, apparently," explained

Macie. She widened her eyes, and her tone became mockingly sincere. "And goodness, Katherine, her daughter could certainly use a friend."

"What's this girl's name?" I asked.

"Leslie Gatlin."

Leslie Gatlin's memorial service must have been the longest thirty-five minutes of my entire life. It felt like ol' Mister Time had just lain down in the road and started dragging himself backward with his lips.

The gym was packed with students and their families, and the choir sang "Amazing Grace" in four-part a cappella harmony. Leslie's mama and daddy sat up in the front row, and the only time I saw them move was when Principal Jenkins introduced Macie Merrick as student body president. Macie walked up to the microphone slow as molasses, and under the giant screen that had Leslie's senior picture projected onto it, Macie gave a version of the speech she had given to the student body. Only, this one was better.

The words were perfectly calculated for the reporters in the back of the room, who would be shooting eyewitness reports on location in the parking lot later. There were quotations and sound bites for days. There was a choked sob behind her voice. There was a single tear that dribbled down her perfectly powdered cheek on the last sentence, and when she stepped away from the mic, it was so silent that you could have heard the clouds scootin' across the sun.

It was the easily the best performance Macie Merrick ever gave, and from where I sat on the raised bleachers, I could tell that she was pleased as punch.

When the service was finally over, Macie made a beeline for the side entrance around the edge of the receiving line where Leslie's parents stood at the front shaking hands and sharing hugs with people they'd never met who were all just happy it wasn't their kid who'd asphyxiated in the garage. Macie was headed out to the vans, and I knew we'd see her again on the six o'clock news. As I was considering this and walking toward the parking lot with Daddy, he stopped and grabbed the hand of a tall, silver-haired man in a well-cut suit. He was younger than his hair color made him seem, maybe forty, and handsome. He wore glasses that had no rims, and the lenses sort of disappeared over his eyes, which were so blue that they almost hollered at you to look at them.

"Kellan Dirkson," Daddy bellowed in his big litigator baritone. "Didn't know you had a high school student at home."

"I don't, Daysun." Kellan smiled. "I'm here working. You remember my associate counsel Lauren Wolinsky? And this is a new addition to the firm, Doug Skovgaard."

"Pleasure to see you, Lauren, and to meet you, Doug." Daddy shook their hands, chuckling. "Working a memorial? What do those ambulance chasers at Latham have you up to now?" Daddy's laughter always sounds like a song.

Mr. Dirkson smiled sadly. "It's a terrible thing, really. We've been retained by the Gatlins to pursue a civil suit for wrongful death."

Daddy's smile fell. "Do they have a case?" he asked quietly.

Kellan Dirkson bit his lower lip and raised his eyebrows as he nodded, then he dropped his gaze and his voice. "Daysun, if half the things this poor girl's mother says are true, it may wind up being a criminal investigation. Bullying is big news lately. You've got half the state legislatures in the country pushing for tougher laws, and our DA is itching to get involved."

Aunt Liza used to tell me there are moments when you know that, because of what just happened, your life will never be the same again. "It's like things take a hard left at Albuquerque," she'd say. "And you realize all a sudden that you're headed to Mexico whether you like it or not."

I don't remember what else Kellan Dirkson and Daddy talked about. Sometimes I lay awake and wonder if there was anything else on earth I could have done at that moment besides pull out my phone and text Beth.

`Where are you?`

11. BETH

The memorial was a nightmare. Mrs. Gatlin was drunk, which I know only because she tottered past me when I was talking to Coach Stevens, and she smelled like champagne. Can't blame her. I was a little jealous. From the time we left the student assembly on Monday morning to the time we showed up at the memorial service on Saturday, I'd spent over fifty hours at school. If I wasn't in class, or cramming for Chem II in the library with Jillian, I was at practice working my floor routine.

And then there were the meetings. When Macie smells opportunity, she can be a spaz—or, as Krista calls it, "A real pain in my ass." This week she was in rare form. If she wasn't texting us about another last-minute meeting to get kids involved in the volunteer effort for the TeenReach Hotline, we were helping her design and print posters for the counseling outreach she'd convinced Principal Jenkins to hire two extra contract guidance counselors for.

It was ridiculous.

And it was working.

People were lining up for counseling sessions, and every time Macie walked by the guidance office, she'd check the sign-up sheet, text her dad's press contacts, and email Principal Jenkins with updates. Jenkins was totally in her hip pocket. He was no dummy. Having the state senator's daughter in student government had been good for the budget.

The truly amazing part was that Macie showed no sign of slowing down. She was a machine. I was so glad when she sat down at the memorial because I thought for sure she'd take the rest of the night off, but just as the choir finished singing, I felt my phone buzz and saw a text that was more of a command than a request:

`Meet you at Marv's after the memorial. Get the booth in the back.`

Krista got the text at the same time. She looked at me and smiled, then squeezed my shoulder. "Let's get back to normal, shall we? This is getting a little maudlin, and I need a cigarette."

She was right. I was so tired of the second-guessing, and jumping every time Macie barked an order. And there was a place right behind my sternum that felt like it was holding a boiling pot of water that might bubble over at any moment.

Last night after practice, I'd scrolled through the messages on Leslie's Facebook wall from the whole week.

The one that she'd posted to me was buried underneath the almost four hundred wall posts that had started the next morning and continued nearly unabated.

No one had commented on it—yet. I was hoping to keep it that way. Surely at some point Facebook would delete the page. Right? Wasn't someone putting up a memorial page? Should I?

I saw Katherine across the gym. She had a pageant tonight, a regional for the Miss Seattle Teen competition. Usually we all went as a group. We were supposed to be there to cheer her on, but usually we just laughed our asses off at the other girls. The lower-level competitions were Macie's favorite. She liked to play the game Find the Biggest Bangs. Tonight I couldn't deal, and I didn't want to have to explain if it came up, so I steered Krista out the side entrance.

As I got into the car, Katherine texted me.

"Who is that?" asked Krista, turning up the radio and checking her lip liner in the mirror above the passenger seat.

"Katherine," I said as I texted her back.

"Where has she been all week?" Krista asked. "She hasn't been at a single one of the student council meetings. You'd think Macie would whip her into line."

I pressed the send button. "I think she's just been busy with pageant stuff," I said. Katherine had been noticeably absent from anything after class hours this week. She'd skipped out on our weekly Brit lit study group during sixth-period study hall on Wednesday, and it had been her turn to outline the chapter. That left us to our own devices for learning the high points about Oscar Wilde. Luckily Josh had been there to give us a crash course.

I couldn't imagine that after everything that had happened already this week, she'd show up to hang out at Marv's when she had a pageant to prepare for.

As we pulled out of our parking space after the memorial, I saw Jillian walking across the parking lot with Jake. His eyes were hidden by sunglasses. I knew from Jills that he was taking this pretty hard.

"Ugh. When is he going to stop moping around?" asked Krista. "He's so much cuter when he smiles."

I didn't say anything. I just turned up the music. Krista has no filter. She says everything she thinks, and she thinks some awful things.

"Think he's coming with Jillian?"

"No," I said. Jake wasn't interested in hanging out with us right now. Of that much I was certain.

12. JAKE

Everything in my head told me not to get into the car with Jillian. I didn't want to hang out after the memorial. I didn't want to pretend that everything was normal. I didn't want to order burgers and shakes and lattes and act like everything was okay.

But I did.

"C'mon, Jake. I know you're having a hard time," Jillian said as we stood in the parking lot at school. "Just come for a little while. Brad's bringing Macie soon."

I couldn't stop from rolling my eyes.

"Jesus!" Jillian sighed. "Would you just lighten up? Get in the car. You'll feel better when you eat something."

She slid into the driver's seat and started flipping through tunes on her iPod. I stood there watching Macie finish up in front of the camera bank. Her dad was standing back by the vans, refusing journalists, waving them over to Macie, and grinning from ear to ear. I felt sick to my stomach. Brad rounded the corner in his truck from the back lot and slowed to a stop when he saw me.

"Hey," he called as he rolled down the window. "You comin' to Marv's?"

I ran a hand over my face and shrugged.

"Come," he said. "Let's get some food with the girls, then we can sneak out when they start planning world domination, and go hang at my place. Dad's outta town all weekend."

I looked over at Macie one more time and then back at Brad. He followed my gaze.

"This is over after today," he said. "Everything will calm down now. See you there, man."

I got in the car, and Jillian pulled out behind Brad, who slowed to pick up Macie. The reporters were packing up. They'd gotten what they'd come for. Macie hugged her grinning dad, who helped her into Brad's truck and gave all of us a two-fingered victory sign like he was delivering a speech on election night, and we headed toward Marv's.

Brad had invited half the football team to come grab food at Marv's, and we all wound up jammed into two big round booths in the back of the place. Macie sat in the center of one, holding court, flanked by Beth and Krista on one side and Jillian on the other. Brad and I took the ends, and both wound up getting up like four times in the first fifteen minutes to let different combinations of the girls out to go to the bathroom together.

Kevin and Brandon, two of our defensive linemen, were with a couple of cheerleaders in the other booth, and the four of them started an all-out spitball war with Brad, who was getting pegged with little wads of napkins they were shooting out of straws. I watched as Beth and Krista joined in to help him out, and before I knew it, everyone was laughing and joking around, and Macie was yelling for all of them to stop it, so they all turned on her and pelted her until she slid down under the table with her hands over her head. Brad hooted like a banshee and high-fived Kevin, and then the waiter showed up with our drinks.

I sat there, dazed, feeling like I was a million miles away. I couldn't remember why I wasn't jumping into the fun. I couldn't remember why my face felt heavy, why it felt like a smile weighed one million pounds.

Then I saw Katherine walk through the door, and I remembered.

When she strode up to the table, I was relieved. She wasn't smiling either. She stopped right in front of us, and she opened her mouth to say something, but Macie beat her to it.

"Well, look who has crawled out of the woodwork," she said with a smirk. "We missed you in front of the cameras today, and come to think of it . . . all week. How is the Pageant Girls Fund for the Prevention of Teen Suicide coming along?"

Krista stifled a laugh. Beth glared at Macie. Jillian glanced at me, her eyes wide. She didn't say anything out loud, but her mental text message came through loud and clear: *Don't. Make. A. Scene.*

The thing I've always liked about Katherine is that she doesn't appear to give a shit what anyone thinks of her. Two years ago when she moved here, I think that's why Macie dumped Jillian as a running mate and went with Katherine—not just because she needed votes, which is what she told Jills. I think it was because Macie recognized a quiet strength in Katherine that she knew she wanted on her side. If she didn't make Katherine a friend, she'd become a challenger.

Katherine was unfazed by Macie's remark. She stood in front of the table and smiled her most runway-ready dazzler. She was beautiful. Nobody could deny it. And not "hot" in the way Kevin and Brandon and Brad talked about the girls on the drill team. Katherine was regal. Her beauty was classic, and there was an energy about her that was unmistakable.

"I trust everyone had a good time at the memorial this morning," she said, an icy tone creeping into her voice as she addressed everyone in both booths. "Macie," she said, leveling her gaze at our booth, "I'm not sure you noticed the two gentlemen in the back set of bleachers. They were with a woman who was recording the service on a Flip Video?"

Macie stared daggers at Katherine. They'd had moments like this in private before. I knew that much from Jills. But I'd never heard of anybody challenging Macie like this in public.

"Katherine, I'm not sure you noticed the two news crews outside? I was talking to the local anchors, who were most certainly not using Flip Videos. They had cameras. They were filming broadcast segments. Maybe you missed that while you were talking to the funeral bloggers?"

Katherine flipped her hair over her shoulder and smiled. "Not bloggers, Macie. Lawyers. Friends of my father's. They work at Latham, Dirkson, and Soloway. Maybe you're wondering what lawyers who didn't know the Gatlins were doing at Leslie's memorial? My father was puzzled by that, too, so he asked."

The waiter rounded the corner with a busboy trailing him. Two giant trays of food arrived. They passed out the plates and asked if there was anything else. Brad managed to mumble, "No thanks; we're good."

No one lifted a fork, or a fry. All eyes were glued on Katherine. Even Macie was paying attention. "What did they tell your dad?" she asked quietly.

"They were hired by the Gatlins," Katherine said slowly. The smile and the iciness of her voice had fallen away. She was just giving us the facts now. "The Gatlins are claiming that Leslie killed herself because of unrelenting bullying. They are gathering evidence to file a civil suit for wrongful death. And they are discussing criminal charges with the district attorney."

The words dropped from Katherine's lips and gently settled

over the table like a thick layer of soot. Everyone else was looking at Katherine. I was looking at Macie.

For the first time since I'd known her, Macie Merrick cracked for just an instant. It was brief, and if I hadn't glanced over at just the right time, I would have missed it—the tiny jump in her lip, the quiver at the edge of her eyelash. The way her lips parted and how she just barely stopped her jaw from dropping.

I had never seen this look on Macie's face before. I'd seen her excited. I'd seen her angry. This was Macie Merrick scared.

It lasted for exactly half a second.

Krista turned to her and said, "What does that mean?" and before she'd gotten the "wh" of "what" out of her mouth, Macie's mask was back in place.

"It means," Macie said, slowly, glaring at Katherine, "that the guilty party is trying to shift the blame."

"The guilty party?" I asked.

"Oh, please, Jake," Macie said with a sneer. "We all know that Mrs. Gatlin is a lush. And who knows what her crazy-ass dad put them through? One of the hallmarks of child molesters is that they like to move around a lot. That man flips a house every year. I don't think they've lived at the same address for more than twelve months in the past decade."

I was on my feet before I could stop myself. The table rocked as I stood up in the booth, and Beth and Jillian leaped to grab their drinks.

"Shut up," I bellowed at Macie. "Just shut up."

Brad and Jillian were on each arm, talking at the same time.

"It's okay, bud," Brad said softly.

"Jake, please," whispered Jillian.

"Please, what?" I looked at Jillian like she'd lost her mind. "Sit here and listen to this bullshit? Did anybody see the Gatlins this morning? Sitting there sobbing in the front row? While . . . *you*," I spat at Macie, "*you* of all people gave a eulogy for their daughter?"

Macie laughed bitterly. "Of course they were crying, you moron. Crying because they know that they're the ones to blame. Who raises a kid to be that selfish? It has to be somebody else's fault. It couldn't possibly be theirs. They need somebody to blame, because the truth that it's their fault is just too horrible to believe."

"Shut up!" I yelled again. I wanted to grab the table and throw it upward toward Macie. I wanted every plate and glass to land in her lap. I wanted her to hurt as badly as I did right that second.

"Jesus, Jake. You're such a little girl," Macie said derisively. "Why are you so upset? Leslie Gatlin didn't want you. She wouldn't date you. You were not a part of her life. Move. On. She obviously did."

"I hope they nail your ass to the wall," I shouted.

The manager was at our table now. "Is there a problem, young man?" he asked me sternly.

"Yeah," I said. "Yeah, there is. We've got a delusional asshole at our table."

"This was a bad idea," Brad said. "Jillian, will you take Macie home? I'm gonna get him outta here."

I pushed Brad off me. "Don't patronize me," I said.

"Young man, one more outburst from you, and I'm calling the police," said the manager. "Now, I suggest you settle up with your waiter and go with your friend here."

I looked back at Macie, who rolled her eyes. "They have no case, Jake. This whole scene will blow over by Monday."

Katherine caught my eye as Brad pushed me toward the door, and as I brushed by her I recognized something in her face. It was a knowing, an understanding—like the kind I used to have with Jillian.

It was a longing, too, a wish that she could be anywhere but here.

I spent the night at Brad's place. Now that his brother, Derek, was at Syracuse, it was just the two of us in his giant house—and sometimes the housekeeper, Paula. His dad was out of town for the weekend, like he had been most weekends since Brad's mom died when we were in seventh grade. Her life insurance settlement had doubled the size of the hedge fund Mr. Wyst managed for the richest tech guys in the Northwest. It also seemed to have doubled the size of the hole in his heart. He tried to fill it nightly with vodka, and usually once a week with some new chick he'd met in Vegas or Tahoe or Mammoth or Los Angeles or San Francisco. Brad and Derek had both gotten some counseling after their mom died, but while their dad paid for their sessions, he never bothered to get any of his own.

Brad got me a beer when we got to his place, and grabbed a copy of our favorite zombie movie. It was one from the last ten years where somebody had finally made zombies fast. There were decades of zombie movies where the people who got eaten by them could've run circles around them, and those totally cracked us up.

We fell asleep on the couches in the media room, and when I woke up the next morning, I went into the bathroom downstairs and splashed some water on my face. It was funny—I didn't look any different, but I felt like I didn't recognize the guy in the mirror. I heard the doorbell ring, and figured it was Paula, who usually checks in on Brad once during the weekend. I went back into the media room and grabbed my T-shirt, then ran up the stairs as the doorbell rang again.

I opened the door as I was pulling my shirt over my head, and froze with one arm in because it was not Paula.

There was a tall, leggy blonde standing on the front porch, gazing out at the front lawn. Black seams ran down the backs of her legs from the hem of her suit skirt. The soles of her high-heel shoes were bright red, and she turned and smiled as she heard the door open. The aviator sunglasses she pushed up on top of her head pulled her long hair back like she was Jennifer Aniston working for the CIA.

"Hi." She smiled. Perfect teeth, dark brown eyes that floated from my face down to my chest and abs. She cocked her head and glanced back up with a smirk as I remembered that my shirt was half off and quickly shoved my other arm in. "Bradley Wyst?"

"Uh . . . hi . . . yeah, I mean, no . . . I'm . . . ," I stuttered, and then stopped.

"Confused?" She laughed—but it was sweet, not bitchy.

I smiled and felt my cheeks burn. "Sorry." I laughed. "I'm Brad's friend. This is his house."

She smiled. "I'm Lauren Wolinsky. Is Bradley Wyst here?"

"Sure thing," I said, holding open the glass storm door. "I'm Jake. C'mon in. I'll get him."

Brad was coming up the stairs in the foyer behind me. In his boxers. "Hey, Pau—"

"Dude." I cut him off.

At the sight of Lauren Wolinsky, Brad let out a long whoosh of air with a frown, then folded his arms over his bare chest and leaned against the door to the stairway.

"You're . . . definitely not the housekeeper."

Lauren Wolinsky pursed her lips in a smirk and shook her head as she reached into a black leather attaché case that hung from the shoulder of her navy suit jacket. "No, no I am not," she said. Then she turned back to me. "Jake . . . as in Jacob Walker?"

"Yes?" I said. Confused but pleased. *She knows my name?*

"Bradley Wyst?"

"You got it," said Brad, extending his hand with the grin he refers to as "the Dazzler."

Lauren offered each of us an envelope and smiled kindly as we took them from her. "Gentlemen, I'm Lauren Wolinsky with Latham, Dirkson, and Soloway. You've been served."

Then she turned on the heel of her red-soled shoe and left us standing there wide awake.

13. JILLIAN

"Jake, I need you to be here," I said again.

I was begging now. The Merricks were due here in fifteen minutes, but he wasn't listening. He pulled on a tank top and bent over to lace up his running shoes.

"Please?" I tried again. He grabbed his Nano and untangled the earbuds. He heard me, but he wasn't listening. He'd barely said a word to me since Saturday, when we met up at Marv's after Leslie's memorial. He stayed at Brad's that night and Sunday night, and today, by the time he got home from practice, we all knew that nothing had blown over with the Gatlins and their lawyers.

"Please, Jake?" I asked again. He finished with his shoes and then reached for his iPod.

I grabbed a pillow off his bed and threw it at his head. "Argh! Jake! I hate it when you give me the silent treatment. Say something!"

Slowly he bent down and put the pillow neatly back onto the bed, then walked to the door. He paused in the hallway, looked back at me, and shook his head.

"There's nothing left to say, Jills. You got yourself into this mess."

"But you're a part of this story too," I said, panic rising in my throat.

"Maybe," he said quietly, looking down at his shoes. "But I didn't write the ending. You and Macie did that. You're on your own."

And then he was gone.

Thirty minutes later, Macie had arrived with her mom and dad and we were all upstairs, waiting on Jake.

"Where's your brother?" Macie's voice was clipped and her jaw was clenched.

"Yeah, Jillian," said Josh with a smirk. "Macie needs some eye candy. She's bored with Brad's ugly mug."

Brad laughed and punched him in the shoulder. "Shut up, asshole."

Josh got a subpoena the same time that Krista and I did. We were on our way to lunch off campus today.

"We have to strategize about this," Macie said from her perch on the arm of the couch, next to Brad. She had her legs crossed and her dangling foot was shaking up and down a million times a second like it does when she's figuring things out.

"Calm down, babe." Brad rested his hand gently on Macie's back.

Our parents were downstairs discussing the subpoenas. Katherine's dad had an associate named Patrick who was going to handle the case for all of us. Mr. Merrick just wanted it kept off the Action News at eleven. Beth's mom wanted it kept off the prayer chain at her church Bible study.

Brad was trying to keep us all off the ceiling. I felt relieved somehow that he was in the room, even though he'd put his hand on Macie's back and not mine. He made me feel settled on the inside, but somehow he made Macie more riled up.

"Don't tell me to calm down, Brad." She shrugged his hand off her back, stood up, and paced over to the window. Brad didn't follow her with his gaze, just looked directly at me and let out a long, slow sigh.

I pursed my lips into almost a smile that said, "We'll get through this."

Then I noticed Katherine staring at Brad staring at me, and I couldn't make out the look that crossed her face, but whatever it was, I didn't feel calm anymore.

Out of the corner of my eye, I saw Macie standing by the windowsill where I kept my snow globe collection. She was staring out onto the driveway and down the street. I could see Jake several blocks away, running toward the house, and I knew Macie saw him, too. She slowly dropped her eyes to the snow globes, and I saw her brush her long, perfect nails over the one from Vegas. My Granny and Gramps had brought it back for me when they went on their annual blackjack trip last Christmas. Macie rolled it slowly back and forth in her hands while Beth started to tear up. Krista heard her sniff and rolled her eyes.

"What?" Beth said too loudly. "What, Krista? I'm the one who has to go first.

"Oh, brother," Krista groaned. "What are you so freaked out about?"

"I'm freaked out because I was on a balance beam when this dude in a suit walked in and handed me a subpoena."

"Yeah, and I got mine in the parking lot, and Katherine got hers at a salon," Krista ticked off in her bored voice. "It's been a long week and it's only Monday. Get over yourself."

Beth started crying, and Katherine sighed. "Oh, for heaven's sake. Daddy's friend is gonna take good care of you, sweetheart," she said, and reached across to pat Beth's leg.

"Hope you're right," said Brad absently, and something in Katherine snapped.

"Hope is not a strategy, Brad." Her nostrils flared as her eyes shot daggers into his. "These are the best lawyers in the Northwest. You can rest assured that their preparations for the depositions will be founded on facts."

"But what am I going to say when they ask me about stuff and Leslie and the Facebook messages?" Beth was in hysterics now; her face was red from crying.

"You're just going to tell them the truth," said Katherine.

"That we were so mean to Leslie that she killed herself?" Beth choked out.

"What?" Krista scoffed. "Would you stop acting like she was the victim here? We're not the ones to blame; it's her parents who missed the boat here."

"Still," I said, "it's good to be prepared. I mean, who knows what they've been able to dig up on Facebook and stuff."

"They can't do that, can they?" Josh asked. "I mean, they can't just call Facebook and get our profiles or anything, right?"

"Yes, Josh," said Katherine sternly. "They can subpoena everything, including, but not limited to, the kitchen sink, and they don't have to tell you about it until you're in the room at the deposition."

"That's total crap," Josh said.

"Well, it's the truth," said Katherine.

"Oh my God—," cried Beth. "What are we going to do?"

"Everybody calm down," Brad said, louder this time.

"Would you stop saying that?" Krista yelled back. "Jesus."

"Why don't you stop talking?" Brad said to Krista. "You don't know what's going to happen until you get into the room, Beth, so there's no sense in crying about it now."

Beth glared at Brad, her face flushed, the tears on her cheeks unable to quell the fire in her eyes. "Excuse me for being the only one who has any feelings about this," she yelled at Brad. "Maybe it doesn't make a difference to anyone else, but I've got one shot at college and I doubt the athletic department at UCLA looks too kindly on wrongful death charges or depos—"

"*Shut up!*" roared Macie, and I glanced back at her just in time to see the Vegas snow globe leave her hand and sail across the couches before it slammed into the door to the media room and shattered in a spray of water and plastic shards.

Katherine and Krista jumped about four feet off the couches, Brad leaped to his feet, and Josh pressed himself up against the wall next to the window Macie was standing in front of. Finally, there was silence in the room. Beth didn't even dare to sniff.

"Good." Macie smiled. "Now that I have your attention, I'm going to give you all the strategy you need."

She walked slowly to the middle of the two couches and stared at Beth.

"Beth, honey, do you know what time it is?"

Beth frowned, then looked down at her phone.

"Four thirty," she said.

"Wrong answer," Macie said, flinging a finger toward the ceiling. "The first thing you learn about spinning is to control the conversation. Control the information."

Without looking back over her shoulder, she pointed at Josh. "Josh! Do you know what time it is?"

We all turned to look at him.

A slow smirk crept across his face. "Yes," he answered. We waited for him to tell her the time.

He didn't. Instead, he folded his arms with a self-satisfied grin.

"Excellent," said Macie with a smile at Beth. "Someone has been watching their *Law and Order*." She knelt down on the floor in front of Beth, taking Beth's face in both hands.

"Beth, honey, when you walk into that room with that lawyer friend of Katherine's dad, you're going to answer questions as vaguely as possible. You're going to answer exactly what they ask, not what they want to know."

She stood up and walked toward the door. "That goes for everyone. If they ask you if you sent this Facebook message, you don't remember, you can't say for sure, it was a long time ago, it was an inside joke, everyone knew it wasn't serious."

She looked at each one of us in turn. "Got it?"

The silence was thick. "We aren't the bad guys here," Macie said. "We are the scapegoats. Leslie's parents want someone to blame. We're going to make sure they don't have to look any farther than the bathroom mirror."

"Macie?" We heard Mr. Merrick in the hallway, then he was at the door.

"Yes, Senator?" Macie said with her on-camera charm.

Her dad poked his head into the media room. "Hey, guys." He grinned. "Everything okay up here? Thought I heard something fall off a shelf."

I jumped up and started picking up the pieces of snow globe. "Oh, we had a little snow globe accident." I laughed.

"Well, thank God." Mr. Merrick chuckled. "Woke me up. Bored outta my mind down there."

There was something about his smile that wasn't right.

"You kids are gonna be fine," he said. "Katherine, your dad's partner is a genius. You've all got nothing to worry about. You'll be ready to go."

"We were discussing a little strategy of our own." Macie smiled. "Meet you at the car in five?"

"Sure thing," he said. He raised two fingers to make a V, then flashed us his trademark campaign smile and walked back down the hallway.

"Give them nothing," Macie said softly. "Meeting adjourned."

Katherine was out the door before anyone else, followed by Beth, then Krista. Josh pecked me on the cheek. "Thanks for hosting, Jills. Tell your brother I said hi."

Brad grabbed his hand like he was shaking it, making sure his arm was between them when they hugged, in that weird way straight guys hug. "Good to see you, bro," he said. "Let's hang soon."

When Josh was gone, Brad headed into the bathroom off my bedroom. "Gotta pee," he said.

"Thanks for the information." Macie sighed.

When he closed the door, she turned to look at me.

"What's up?" she asked.

"I'm worried," I said.

"Why?" she asked.

"Jake has a subpoena too."

"Of course he does," she said. "He was the last person to talk to her alive."

"But it's not only that," I explained. "I think he's going to tell them everything. I mean, he was the closest thing Leslie had to a friend. What do we do if he brings it up in his deposition?"

Macie smiled at me blankly. "Brings what up?"

The bathroom door opened. I could hear Brad walking back into the room behind me.

"You know . . . ," I began.

"Hey, babe." Brad spun Macie to him, wrapping his arms around her waist and pulled her up toward him for a sweet, soft kiss. "Call me later?"

She nodded and he held her. He looked over her shoulder and winked at me without smiling.

This was the group hug we'd all shared since ninth grade. We'd been saying good-bye like this for three years now.

Macie got his arms.

I got his eyes.

I wished I knew for sure who had his heart.

14. KATHERINE

Once a week after school I drove over to Daddy's office, and usually he handed me a stack of documents to file and we talked about a case. He knew I had my eye on Harvard Law, and we'd been doing this since I was in seventh grade.

On Wednesday morning I asked Daddy if I could stop by today instead of on Thursday. Macie wanted to see Beth's deposition as soon as possible.

"Sho', princess," he said. "You really wanna come back for more after the grillin' Patrick gave y'all yesterday during witness prep?"

"Oh, yes, sir." I smiled and winked. "You fixin' to lose me to Harvard next fall. My hourly rate will be too high to ever work for you again."

He laughed, and I was relieved. *One more day of laughing,* I thought. *Just one.* Somewhere down inside me I knew that once the depositions started, he wouldn't be laughing anymore.

Witness preparation had been a joke. We'd all been there together, so claiming we had no idea what was going on worked on some level. None of us was going to crack in front of everybody else. Macie was really good as far as denying everything Patrick threw at her, but she was clearly annoyed around the edges—little things, her foot started bouncing. She still had that news camera smile, but you could tell she was ruffled. She was used to standing up when she was selling something. Sitting down made her fidgety.

Jillian was a wide-eyed sweetheart, but her face answered every question before she even opened her mouth, and Krista looked shifty, period. Poor Beth was a mess. She started crying on the third question, and Daddy and I had to walk her around in the parking lot to calm her down.

In a strange way I was the best witness we had. I used Aunt Liza's poker face. I smiled at the beginning, was serious in the middle, and said thank you at the end.

"Ladies, that's the way it's done," said Patrick when he turned off the camera. "Nice work, Katherine."

When I got to Daddy's office at about four thirty, I asked him if he'd seen the footage of Beth's deposition yet. He grabbed the video camera from Patrick's office and plugged it into my laptop so I could watch, instead of simply handing it over to Macie. Then he headed down the hall to a last-minute meeting with a client over a disputed permitting process.

The video loaded and popped open in QuickTime. The shot was on Beth—looking down at her hands, biting her lip. I clicked play.

Beth sat next to Patrick and faced Kellan Dirkson and Lauren Wolinsky, who I remembered meeting at Leslie's memorial. Kellan's kind, blue eyes matched his smile as he handed Beth and Patrick bottles of water, then turned to Lauren and asked, "Shall we get started?"

She nodded and looked to Patrick, who swept his brown bangs off his forehead and flipped open a legal pad, then looked at Beth.

"Ready?" he asked.

She looked up at him, then over at Kellan and Lauren, and gave a short nod.

She was terrified, and watching the scene unfold, I had a sinking feeling in my stomach.

This was over before it even began.

Lauren started by having Beth raise her hand and solemnly swear to tell the truth, the whole truth, and nothing but the truth. And somehow Beth did this pleasantly, with a smile, direct eye contact—the whole thing, like Patrick had coached us.

Then she turned to Kellan and he asked her to state her name for the record.

"Beth Patterson," she said.

He had her identify Leslie in a picture. She pointed. He smiled.

"Thank you, Miss Patterson. When did you first meet Leslie Gatlin?"

"The summer before freshman year," she said.

"Were you friends with Leslie?"

"Back when I first met her?" Beth asked, looking confused. She glanced over at Patrick.

"Were you friends with her at all?" asked Kellan.

Beth paused. Kellan smiled kindly at her, and I saw her warm up to him like she was scootin' up to a hot fire on a cold night.

"Yes . . . ," she said cautiously. "Back when we first met. We were . . . friends."

"Were you aware of the rumor that was started about Leslie during the first few weeks of her freshman year?" Kellan's smile was gone. He was all business.

Beth frowned and looked at Patrick. He nodded toward Kellan, indicating that she should answer the question.

"I don't know what rumor you're talking about," she said. Slowly her cheeks were flushing.

"The first one we have record of was in regards to Leslie having had breast implants." Kellan's face was stone. "Did you have knowledge of this rumor?"

"I . . ." Beth opened her mouth, then stopped, flustered. "It was three years ago," she said, turning to Patrick. "Why are we talking about this?"

Kellan took a sip of water and offered a tight-lipped smile.

"Miss Patterson, we're in the part of a legal case called discovery. We're trying to discover the facts regarding any involvement you or your classmates may have had in the wrongful death of Leslie Gatlin."

"But I . . ."

"Yes or no, Miss Patterson? Did you ever hear a rumor about Leslie Gatlin having breast implants? And might I remind you that you are under oath."

Beth's hand trembled as she unscrewed the cap on her water bottle and took a sip.

"Yes," she said softly. "I heard that rumor."

"Did you ever repeat this rumor to anyone else?"

Beth glanced over at the court reporter, who sat looking back at her, fingers poised over the black levers, waiting.

"I don't see what this has to do with anything."

"Miss Patterson, we are attempting to establish a pattern of unrelenting bullying over a period of time. I'll ask you again, did you ever repeat the rumor you heard about Miss Gatlin?"

"I don't know why you would accuse me of repeating a rumor like that three years ago. I was Leslie's friend then."

"So, do I understand that you did not repeat the rumor, Miss Patterson?"

"No—*no*! You don't understand." Beth was sobbing now, and as her tears fell harder, Patrick put a hand on her arm and requested a five-minute break.

Beth shook his hand off her arm. "I don't need a break. I

need you to understand what it's like," she shot back at Kellan. "You have no idea what it's like, do you? You can sit here behind your big white table and take your notes and try to trip us all up, but you don't have any idea what it's like to be a girl in high school, do you?"

Kellan took a different tack. "Miss Patterson, you've stated that you were friends. Did you ever have a romantic relationship with Leslie Gatlin?"

"Objection. Relevance." Patrick was not happy.

Lauren Wolinsky slid an iPad across the table toward Beth.

"Have you ever seen this Facebook wall post, Miss Patterson?"

Beth glanced at the screen. "Yes," she said.

"Please read it out loud for the record."

Beth sighed, then read: "'List Chick, I'm sorry I didn't feel the same way about you. I could've been your friend. Anchors away.'"

"Beth, who is List Chick?"

"I don't know!" Beth's eyes were a little wild. She was desperate.

Kellan picked up a piece of paper and slid it across the table to Patrick.

"Exhibit twelve-A. This is a printout from Miss Patterson's Gmail account. You'll notice that it is a Facebook notification message sent to the email address listchick1@gmail.com."

He turned back to Beth. "Miss Patterson, is this your email address?"

Beth hung her head. "Yes."

Kellan nodded. "Beth, did you ever express interest in dating Miss Gatlin?"

"Objection! Relevance." Patrick's face was a storm cloud.

"Just trying to establish a motive for consistent slander and harassment of Leslie Gatlin via Facebook messages," explained Kellan.

He handed a stack of paper to Patrick.

"Exhibit twelve-B. These are printouts of hundreds of messages subpoenaed from a Facebook profile with the name of Di Young. These messages were sent from several IP addresses traced to three different residences. One of them is Miss Patterson's. Beth, did you ever send a Facebook message to Leslie Gatlin from this account?"

Beth was silent and stared at her hands.

"Miss Patterson?" Kellan leaned forward.

"Beth, answer the question," said Patrick.

"Yes."

"Did you set up the account under the name Di Young?" asked Kellan.

"It wasn't my idea. I—"

"Yes or no?" Kellan interrupted her forcefully.

Beth paused and sucked in her cheeks. Her eyes filled with tears. She glanced at Patrick, who stared down at the stack of printouts, looking pale.

"Yes," she sighed.

"Beth, why did you turn on Leslie Gatlin?" Kellan asked quietly.

"You don't get it, do you?" Her voice was too loud for the tiny room. Tears streamed down her face.

"Beth." Patrick's voice was firm. "Let's take a break. You're getting emotional."

"Yeah, I'm getting emotional," she spat out in frustration. "Nobody understands how hard it is. If you're a guy, you can be good at sports and get away with anything, but if you're a girl in sports, it's all different. You've got to keep the rumors at bay. If you're too good, you're a dyke or a bitch, plain and simple. And all it takes is one rumor—one wrong word by the right person—and your whole life is over."

The court reporter was wide-eyed and her fingers were dancing on those levers like the feet of the organist at our old church in Atlanta.

In the silence that followed, Lauren Wolinsky pulled some tissues out of her attaché case and gently handed them across the table to Beth.

"No further questions," said Kellan with a smile.

The video ended on Patrick holding his head in his hands.

15. BETH

After my deposition, Patrick walked me to the empty front lobby.

"Is your mom picking you up?" he asked.

"No. She's hosting Bible study tonight," I said. "Why?"

"Just wanted to touch base with her. Where are you off to now?"

"The gym." I laughed a little bitterly. "Nothing's as good for your floor routine as a deposition."

Patrick plopped down on the couch by the door and rubbed his temples. "Have a good practice," he said.

I stood there waiting for him to move, but he didn't.

"That's it?" I asked quietly.

He looked up at me. "What?" he asked.

I threw my bag down. "That's it? Just 'have a good practice'? We aren't going to discuss what just happened in there?"

Suddenly he was sitting up, his forearms on his knees, leaning toward me. "I don't know, Beth. Are we?" he shot back. "Let me explain something to you. The only thing I'm interested in discussing is the truth here. Your parents are potentially on the hook for hundreds of thousands of dollars here—and that's if this thing settles out of court. If we go to trial, the number goes up."

I stared at the floor.

"I'm waiting," he said.

"For what?" I asked.

"Look, you want to discuss what just happened in there, I'm all ears. But I don't have time to dick around unless you're going to tell me the truth. You all but perjured yourself in there just now, and even though you didn't technically lie, you gave Dirkson exactly what he wanted—you on the ropes, covering up God knows what for God knows who. So, go ahead, have a great practice. Nail that dismount tonight. Because when this thing winds up in court, you're gonna be walking a balance beam you've never trained for. And the only way I can help you is if you get real and tell me what the hell is going on here."

"I'm late for practice," I said, picking up my bag.

"Beth." The way he said my name stopped me in my tracks. "Look at me."

I turned and faced him.

"I know that this wasn't all you. I know that you were

actually Leslie's friend at some point. What happened?" He was begging me to tell him the truth.

"What could possibly be so horrible that you'd have to keep it a secret?"

"I have to go," I said, and I pushed through the office doors and outside.

By the time I got to the gym, Coach Stevens had already started practice. When he saw me come out of the locker room, he shouted some instructions at an assistant coach and headed toward me.

"Had your deposition today?"

I nodded.

"How'd it go, Beth?"

"Fine," I said, wrapping my left wrist.

"I don't know how this started, Beth," Coach Stevens said quietly. "I wish I knew." Then he walked me over to the uneven parallel bars and gave me a lift.

It all started after the cookout at Coach Stevens's place. After we met at her uncle's place, Leslie and I started spending a lot of time together. One Saturday before school started, she insisted that I come with her to Jake's for guitar lessons.

"C'mon." She smiled as we rolled our bikes out of her garage. "It'll be good for you to know *somebody* besides me on the first day."

"Well, yeah," I said, "but . . . isn't this sort of like your once-a-week guitar date?" I giggled. "I don't want to be a third wheel."

Leslie rolled her eyes. "This is not a date. We're just . . ."

"Making beautiful music together?" I smirked.

"Enough. Ride."

And we did. And she was right. I'd never met anybody like Jake. He was so good-looking and so nice at the same time. No one could feel like a third wheel around him. When he smiled, you felt like you belonged.

"Where's Jillian?" Leslie asked when we got there.

"Pro'ly at Macie's," Jake said.

"Who's Macie?" I asked them.

"You may remember her from such election-night coverage as last year's race for the state senate and the previous race for the mayor's mansion," Jake quipped.

Leslie giggled and playfully punched him in the shoulder. "Be nice!"

"You mean Macie . . . Merrick?" I asked. "She goes to school with you guys?"

"Oh, yes," sighed Jake. "We're truly blessed. She and Jillian are planning a wholesale takeover of student government even as we speak, one class presidency at a time."

"Really?" asked Leslie through her laughter.

"They've turned the study at the Merrick mansion into a war room," Jake said.

"Shut up," I said, giggling. "Really? That's hilarious."

"Oh, it's no laughing matter," Jake said. "Serious as flesh-eating bacteria. Wait till you meet her at the Frosh Bash."

"The what?" Leslie and I said it at the same time.

Jake laughed. "Two weeks. Sunday afternoon, Labor Day weekend. Brad Wyst's place. His older brother, Derek, is a senior this year. He's inviting everybody who's anybody. My mom will drive. I'll pick you two up."

When we got back to Leslie's house after her guitar lesson with Jake, she bent over to hoist her bike up onto the hook in her garage, and the necklace she'd shown me the first time we met fell out of her tank top, the tiny silver anchor dangling over her chest. I stared at it for a moment, swinging there, and when she glanced up, I looked away a moment too late. I felt myself blush. Hard.

"Ugh." She laughed. "I know. I had to go buy all new sports bras for volleyball with my mom last week. It's like I've got grapefruits slamming me in the chin now when I run."

I laughed nervously. "Sorry, I didn't mean to stare. Your necklace fell out, and then I . . . noticed."

"Yeah, no shit." Leslie rolled her eyes. "The busboys at Marv's have suddenly realized I'm alive. Guys are so stupid like that."

"Jake doesn't seem so stupid," I said.

"Yeah." She smiled. "He's nice. And he really liked you, I could tell."

"So, have you kissed him since the beach?" I asked.

"No!" Leslie laughed. She said it like we were in fourth grade and boys had cooties. She shook her head with a little shiver. "It's not like that with us."

"What do you mean?" I asked her. "He seems pretty smitten."

"We were at a beach in the moonlight on vacation," she said matter-of-factly. "He's like my brother."

"He doesn't look at you like you're his sister," I said. "And you guys have those necklaces."

"We all got one," Leslie said, tucking the anchor back into her tank top and adjusting her straps. I followed the curve of her shoulder and felt a twinge in my chest—my much smaller chest. "Jillian's has a ship's wheel. Jake's has a sailboat. We got them at this little tourist shop on the shore."

"Well, you're lucky that you'll have something to show off at that pool party," I said.

She frowned. "My . . . necklace?"

"No, silly. Those great big *boobs*!" I lunged at her and tickled her. She shrieked and spun around, trying to wiggle away from my hands. We tangled up against her mom's Audi and stopped when she was finally able to grab my wrists. Leslie's back was up against the car.

How did I get so out of breath from trying to tickle her?

"All I know is that if you sprouted those things on the gymnastics team, you'd have to retrain on all the apparatus," I said.

"Gymnasts have tiny racks for a reason. It's a blessing and a curse."

"Whatever, Beth." Leslie laughed. "You're perfect."

It was suddenly very quiet. Her lips were close enough to my face that I could smell her coconut lip balm. I felt the warmth of her body, the nearness to mine.

I wanted to be closer to her. All at once, I felt a rush in my heart and my chest, and I leaned in and touched my lips to hers.

"Whoa! Beth—wait. What are you doing?" Leslie giggled and spun away from the car, away from my kiss.

Away from me.

I felt my cheeks flush a deep crimson, and the back of my neck felt hot. I stared at the floor, frozen. My heart was racing and I felt dizzy, like I needed to sit down before I fell down. I slowly sank down onto the concrete floor of the garage, overwhelmed by the twist of fear in my stomach.

"Beth."

It was Leslie. She was slowly kneeling next to me on the garage floor.

"Beth?"

I couldn't answer her. I couldn't look at her.

"Beth, it's okay."

It's not okay. You were never supposed to see that part of me.

We sat in silence. I stared at the floor. I made a list. A list of the people who could never know about this moment. I would never reach the end.

"Beth, are you a lesbian?"

She asked it quietly, and like it was no big deal, but when she said that word, something in me snapped.

"Don't say that word," I hissed.

I leaped to my feet. She tried to stop me and I pushed her away. I ran toward the door that led into the house. I wanted to get my things and keep running as far away as I could. All the hope I had felt since that night at Coach Stevens's cookout, when I lay next to Leslie on the hood of her dad's truck and looked at the stars, vanished.

I was so sure.

Leslie followed me to the front door. "Beth? It's okay. I won't tell anyone about this. I swear."

My eyes narrowed. "You'd better not."

"Call me later?"

I pushed out the front door with a single word:

"No."

After Jake's mom picked up Leslie for the Frosh Bash, she drove by my place to get me. Jake jumped out of the passenger seat in the Range Rover and held the door for me to climb in. I was relieved that I wouldn't have to sit in the back next to Leslie. I could feel her eyes on me as we drove into the Wysts' circular drive.

I couldn't believe how stupid I'd been to kiss her. I hated her for not wanting me, and now she knew something about me that no one else could know. How could I be seen with her when I met all the kids I'd be attending school with? I would never be able to trust her.

Ever.

As we stepped out of the car in front of Brad's house, I thought I might throw up.

"Oh. My. God," Leslie said, staring up the house.

"I know. Ridic, right?" Jake said as he bounded up the porch stairs. "Bradley's dad developed the whole subdivision. Get in here—I'll give you the grand tour."

The house was staggering. The subdivision was called Medina, something I learned from the framed plat map that took up an entire wall of Mr. Wyst's study on the second floor. Of course, that was after we'd seen the media room, five bedrooms, and the giant kitchen filled with warm hardwoods and rough-hewn marble countertops. Two silver dishwashers matched a gleaming stainless range that had enough oven space for an entire pig, and a refrigerator the size of my bedroom.

Brad had asked Jake to come over early to help him set up, and when we stepped into the hot August sun at the pool, Brad was on the far side with a skimmer, talking on his cell phone. He smiled and waved at us, then turned away to finish his call.

"Shh," said Jake with a finger to his lips. Then he kicked off his flip-flops and started running toward the end of the pool, whipping off his baseball cap and tank top along the way.

When he reached the diving board, he took a huge bounce, followed by an arching gainer that he landed in a cannonball, sending a wave of water perfectly aimed to nail Brad with optimum splash.

"Dude."

It was all Brad said, in a perfect understatement, standing there drenched from head to toe. He flicked the water off his phone, then spoke into it again.

"I gotta go. Jake just got here with a couple of total babes."

Brad was grinning at us when he said this—only, not leering, smiling. It was a nice smile—almost shy. He tossed his phone onto a stack of towels and peeled off his wet T-shirt, then dove directly at Jake's head in the deep end. While they wrestled each other under the water for the next three minutes, I stood next to Leslie, watching her laugh at the antics in the pool. She looked fantastic.

Better than I did.

At that instant, I saw two girls coming out the back door. One had Jake's beautiful eyes, and long, wavy chestnut locks.

That must be Jillian.

The girl she was with I recognized from the news coverage of election nights past. Macie Merrick had arrived. I made a beeline for them. I didn't know what I would say, but I knew one thing for certain.

I was going to get to them before Leslie did.

16. JAKE

Brad and I were pulling into a parking place at Scarecrow Video when I realized I felt happy—but I wasn't sure why. Of course, the minute I was aware that I was happy again, I realized that it was because I'd forgotten that Leslie didn't work here anymore. She wouldn't be standing behind the counter when I went up to rent the next zombie movie Brad and I were going to watch. She wouldn't have a suggestion or try to trick me into taking home a "classic."

I sat in Brad's truck wondering where the tears had gone. I wasn't sure when they ran out, only that there weren't any left, and that felt sadder than knowing she was dead: knowing that my feelings were changing already—like with each day, the memory of what Leslie had meant to me faded a little more.

Brad must have sensed it.

"You just remembered, huh?"

I was quiet and looked out the window at the building.

Brad started to laugh. I spun around and glared at him. "What the hell, man?"

He raised both his hands in defense and giggled harder. "No—no, dude. Wait. I'm—I'm sorry. I . . . damn. I was thinking about that first day I met Leslie and Beth. Remember? At the Frosh Bash?"

He dissolved into laughter and it was infectious. I smiled and shook my head. Brad was wiping his eyes. "Holy shit." He laughed. "Macie didn't know what hit her."

There was a surge in my chest when he said it, and the picture of Leslie snapped into sharp focus in my head. The feelings were back—all of them this time. Not only the sadness but the warmth of the sun on my neck at the pool and the cold splash of the water as I climbed out of the pool that day at Brad's three years ago and saw Leslie slip out of her T-shirt and kick off her sandals.

Macie and Jillian arrived a good half hour before everybody else. And by "everybody else" I mean the who's who of the cool kids at Westport. Derek delivered. Anyone who was on a sports team or pretty or popular was there.

There were plenty of girls who were all cute enough, but Leslie was the real star.

"Holy cow," murmured Derek when he walked out onto the deck. She was wearing a new suit I hadn't seen in Cape

Cod: a bright-red two-piece—not a bikini really; it had boy trunks and a cute top that showed just enough. Her hair was slung back in a ponytail. No bows. No makeup. No fuss.

As the pool started to fill up with people, Derek and a couple of other guys fired up the grill. Leslie and I were telling Brad about the surf instructor at the Chatham Bars Inn.

"Yeah." Leslie laughed. "When I asked him what his name was, he said, 'Diego, duuuuuuude.'"

I smiled. "So I was like, 'C'mon, man. What's your real name?' And he was like, 'My friend's call me Diego, duuuuuuuuude.'"

Leslie jumped in: "So then Jillian was all business and said really slowly: 'What . . . did your *mother* . . . name you?'"

At that moment, I felt Jillian's arm around my neck as she peeked over Leslie's shoulder. In her best Diego impersonation, she said, "Umm . . . Charleston."

We all laughed and Leslie hugged Jillian. "Oh my *God*! *Hi!* That was so hilarious. You know he's from this total WASPy blue-blood family. His dad is probably a professor at Harvard."

"Yeah, but you'd never know it from the shaggy blond highlights and the dirty fingernails," I said.

Brad laughed. "Didn't you say he went around barefoot everywhere?"

"Yeah." Jillian snorted. "And after that day he talked us all into surf lessons, he tried to ask Leslie out on a date."

"And who wouldn't, with a rack like that?"

The voice was a guy's and came from behind me. I spun around ready to lay down the law and came nose to nose with Josh Phillips.

"'Sup, bros?" He dropped his voice to a butch Neanderthal's, then handed me and Brad beers.

"Josh!" Jillian jumped across me to Josh for a hug. Brad held up a hand for a high five, but Josh just crossed his arms. "Dude. We're in high school now. High fives are for children."

I laughed as Brad locked an arm around Josh's neck and rubbed his knuckles against Josh's scalp, beer sloshing everywhere.

"This is Josh Phillips," I said, introducing him to Beth and Leslie. "He's got the fastest time for the two hundred butterfly in the state."

Josh was lean but solid. At six foot three he was an inch taller than Brad and I, but weighed twenty pounds less and could outstretch any guy in the Northwest.

"Lovely ladies of the freshman class," he said, tipping his red Wayfarer Ray-Bans and peering over the frames. "Anything to drink?"

"Dry martini, up," said Macie as she slunk into the circle between Brad and me. "You can be the drink boy today, but let's remember it's a service role."

"What the fuck, Macie—?" I started.

Josh held up a hand. "Easy there, Walker. This one doesn't mean any harm; she's just worried I look better in my swimsuit than she does."

Macie smiled. "Or maybe I do mean some harm, Josh. And where are those little Speedos you race in? I was so hoping we'd see them on you today."

"Board shorts today, Ms. Merrick. Didn't want to frighten you, sweetheart," said Josh. "Beth? Jillian? Leslie? To drink?"

"I'll just take a Diet Coke," said Leslie, eager to change the subject.

Jillian glared at Macie. "I'll come with you, Josh."

"Excellent." He smiled. "Macie, I'm afraid we're fresh out of gin, but I'll make some lemonade and see if we can't sweeten up that sour puss of yours."

Bradley howled with laughter as Macie blushed.

"C'mon, Jills," said Josh as he grabbed her hand. "You've just been promoted to assistant mixologist." Then he dragged her over toward the grill and the outdoor kitchen area, where Derek had set up the bar.

"Not cool," I said to Macie when Josh was out of earshot.

"Oh, come now, Jake." Macie fake pouted. "Just reminding everyone of the natural order of things. Can't have the swim boys running amok."

"I see you've met our new gymnast?" I asked.

"Yes indeed," said Macie. "She's cute as a button. Came running right over to introduce herself."

Beth smiled nervously. She seemed to be looking at everyone but Leslie.

"And this is Leslie," I said.

Leslie smiled and extended her hand.

"Oh, I know who you are," said Macie, ignoring her hand and reaching toward her bikini top for the chain around her neck. "Jake! How cute. You and Leslie are wearing your little friendship necklaces. Jillian told me about those."

Leslie fingered the charm around her neck, and I felt my cheeks burn as Macie continued her act.

"I made Jillian take hers off. Can't have the poor girl getting an ugly white blotch in the middle of her chest from that charm."

I saw Leslie's face cloud, and then she composed herself and tried again.

"We had a really great time in Cape Cod," she said to Macie. "It's so beautiful there. We were just talking about the day we took surf lessons and—"

"Oh—huh," Macie said, interrupting her.

"What?" asked Leslie, confused.

Macie reached over and ran a finger along my collarbone, under the silver chain, and suggestively down between my pecs, where the sailboat pendant hung.

"Jake's is a boat and yours is an anchor," she said, looking at Leslie. Then she let out a little chuckle. "How appropriate."

She dropped the sailboat against my chest. "Well, I need to go and say hello to some sophomores. Beth, join us?"

Beth nodded eagerly.

"Nice meeting you, Leslie," Macie said coolly.

She took a few steps and turned back to me, adjusting the sarong that hung from her hips, under her white strapless top.

"Careful of that anchor, Jake. Wouldn't want it tying you down."

"You two never really got along after that," Brad said, staring into the window of Scarecrow Video from his truck.

"We never really got along before that," I said, sliding out of the truck. Brad followed and we walked toward the front door of the store. I saw Andy standing behind the counter. He nodded at me and raised a hand. I waved back.

"Macie felt like you were supposed to be with her. You were always her pick for high school boyfriend. I was second choice."

"I never made Macie any promises, Brad."

"Didn't have to," said Brad. "Macie promised herself that you'd be hers. You're the first thing she ever wanted that she couldn't have."

I reached for the door. "Don't worry. I won't be the last."

17. JILLIAN

Brad texted me from the video store with Jake.

`Hey babe. DVD zombie flix wJake?`

I responded, `Calculus.`

Then the phone rang. It was Katherine. I tapped ignore on my phone and kept working equations.

She called back. I sighed and tapped accept.

"Hey, Katherine," I said.

"What are you doing?" she asked.

"Calculus homework," I said. "I kind of need to get back to it."

"Jillian, I need to talk to you," she said.

I put down my pencil. "Okay. I've got five minutes, then I have to finish this assignment. I need every last brain cell to do it. I completely failed the last pop quiz on Monday. It was right after Dirkson gave us our subpoenas and there was no way I could focus."

"What happened freshman year?"

"What?" I asked. "Freshman year? With who?"

"With everyone," Katherine said. "How did this start?"

"Katherine, this is not a five-minute story."

"Jillian, it's about to be the end of the story if somebody doesn't tell me what's going on. I've never asked 'cause I figured y'all had your own thing goin' before I got here last year, and I certainly didn't need to know what I didn't need to know."

She was quiet for a minute.

"And now you need to know?" I asked.

"Jillian, Beth's deposition . . ." Her voice trailed off, and I felt my stomach seize in a knot the way it used to when I played a piano recital when I was a little girl.

"What about it?" I asked.

"She wasn't . . . ," Katherine started, then stopped herself. "It didn't go very well." She sighed.

"Why are you calling me?" I asked. "Shouldn't we be talking to Macie about this?"

"I'm calling you, Jillian, because I want what I've never gotten from Macie."

"What's that?" I asked.

"The truth."

I looked down at the graph paper lying in the crease of my calculus textbook and thought about all the figuring out I'd had to do over the years with Macie—all the problems, the subtracting of certain facts, the addition of others, the division that resulted.

I was so tired of solving Macie Merrick.

"What do you want to know?" I asked.

"Freshman year," said Katherine. "How did it start?"

I stretched out my legs and leaned back against my headboard, then I closed my eyes, took a deep breath, and told her.

First day of freshman year, Macie stayed over the night before. We made a list of the It Crowd for that year based on the pool party. "Let's review," said Macie. "You, me, Jake, Bradley: freshman class royalty. New girls: Beth—gymnast, undecided cool factor. Leslie—slut who wants Jake."

"Oh, c'mon, Macie. Leslie is not a slut. We had fun on vacation this summer."

"Don't know her. Don't trust her. Did you see the way she hung all over Jake?" Macie scowled. "Just because your parents like her parents doesn't mean she makes the cut."

"I really think she and Jake are just friends," I said.

"They won't be for long," said Macie. "I swear, by the time I'm through with her, he won't know she exists."

Brad walked Macie and me to lunch that first day. As we headed down the stairs, I saw Beth walking ahead of us and called her name. She stopped and turned around. A shy smile crossed her face—almost a look of relief.

"Hi, Jillian," she said. "I was just getting worried about where I was going to sit."

"Well, stay away from that Leslie girl," said Macie. "That's my advice to you. Pretty much any other table will do."

I shot Macie a look. "Come sit with us," I said.

The cafeteria at Westport was gorgeous and new. The whole building had been remodeled and the back of the room was two stories of glass that looked out onto the football field. Trees and a green lawn swept up to the doors, and on nice days like today, the tables on the patio under the trees were filled, too. It looked like the football team was out there, and most of the swim and gymnastic teams as well. The cheerleaders were hovering in between tables on the patio, orbiting the football and basketball players, then touching base at the row of tables just inside the doors.

Jake and Leslie were hanging out by the front doors where we walked in with Beth.

"Hey, you guys!" He waved us over.

"Hi!" Leslie was all smiles. She hugged me and then Brad. Beth fidgeted and looked at the floor. It looked like she was blushing, but I couldn't be sure.

"Where have you been all my life?" Macie asked Jake, ignoring Leslie completely.

"Hanging with the commoners." Jake smiled.

"How about this weekend we get together and see what we have in common?" Macie raised an eyebrow as she threw down the gauntlet.

Jake's sideways smile peaked the corner of his mouth as he shook his head.

"Have to take a rain check on that one, Macie. Chemistry is gonna kill me this semester and we've already got homework. Besides, Leslie and I have a guitar lesson on Sunday, and the rest of the time, I'll be at practice. Brad and I are the new grunts on the team. Have to show 'em we're in shape."

"Speaking of," said Brad, "Derek wants us out on the patio, pronto."

"Duty calls." Jake winked at Leslie. "Call me tonight and let me know what time works for guitar on Sunday."

"See you, Jake's sis . . . ," said Brad with a smile. He knew it drove me crazy when people referred to me in terms of Jake. Like my brother owned me or something.

"Are you talking to me?" I asked.

"Yeah," he said. "Pretty sure I am."

"I'm Jillian," I said, then pointed at Jake. "He would be Jillian's brother."

"Got it," he said with a big grin.

Jake rolled his eyes. "Dude. Did you just use the Dazzler on my sister? Really?"

"Shh!" Brad stage-whispered. "Don't give away the secrets of the big smile." He winked at me as they walked away.

"Well," said Macie, watching them go. "Somebody has an eye out for you, Miss Jillian Walker."

"Oh, whatever." I laughed. Beth smiled. "No, I think she's right, Jillian."

"You two wanna join us?" asked Leslie.

"Oh, we'd love to," said Macie. "But Jillian and I have a ton of work to do in order to be ready for class elections in two weeks."

"Wow!" said Leslie. "Ambitious. I thought about running, but I checked out the website a couple weeks ago and realized there's not much time to build a platform—especially when you're new."

"Yeah," said Macie with a weird smile. "It's easier when you have a little brand recognition going for you already."

"Well, good luck," Leslie said. "If you need any help, I'll be over at Jake and Jillian's this weekend. I'd be happy to pitch in making posters or whatever you need."

I opened my mouth to say thanks, but before I could, Macie jumped in. "Coming, Beth?" Her question was a command.

Beth sprang forward to follow us, and as she did, I saw Leslie's face fall. I knew she was hurt. Macie had claimed me, and now she was taking Beth. As we left Leslie alone at the door, I managed a smile and a wave over my shoulder before tripping into the corner of a table as Macie dragged me away.

"Ow! Macie? What was that?" I asked.

"Sorry, ladies," she said, addressing with a smile the girls at the table I'd smacked into.

"No worries," said a girl with short bangs cut straight across her forehead. Her bloodred lips and nails matched her trendy, vintage cat's-eye glasses. "Hey, you're Macie Merrick, aren't you?"

"Sure am," Macie said. "I'm also *starving*, which is why I tried to drag Jillian here through your table instead of around it. Low blood sugar hampers my depth perception."

"My parents voted for your dad for mayor. I'm Krista," she said.

"Awesome," said Macie. "Totally great. Are you freshmen?" she asked.

All four of the girls nodded.

"Even better," said Macie. "I'm running for class president, and Jillian here is going to be my VP candidate."

"That's so cool," said Krista. "Hey, do you know that girl that you were just talking to?"

"Not really," said Macie.

The girl with the red hair sitting next to Krista piped up. "Oh, that's too bad. I was hoping you could introduce us. That girl with the blond hair is so pretty."

Macie cocked her chin and raised her eyebrows. "Well, isn't that sweet. And your name is . . . ?"

"Kelly," she said, extending her hand.

Macie shook it. "Well, ladies, anyone can be that pretty."

"What do you mean?" Krista laughed. "I'll never look like that. That doesn't just happen overnight."

"It most certainly does," said Macie.

Blank stares—all around.

"Oh, puh-leease," Macie scoffed. Then, in a conspiratorial whisper, she added, "Do you really think that puberty is that gracious to anyone? Those tits are a hundred percent silicone."

"Really?" Kelly's eyes were wide like lightbulbs. "Whose mom would let them do that?"

"You're kidding, right?" said Macie with a stifled laugh. "Have you seen her mom's rack? Linda Gatlin, real estate agent. Google her on the way to fifth period. Same doctor did the surgery. And from what I hear, Leslie paid for those in person."

"Wow. Impressive," said Krista. "Where did she get the money?"

"Who said anything about money?" Macie asked, a gleam in her eyes. "Apparently, the doctor got a great deal on a house and had a special buy-one-get-one-free deal for a mother/daughter combo."

"Oh my God," said Kelly.

The girl across the table from her let out an "Ew!" while the other slowly slid her phone out of her purse and started sending a text.

"You're joking," said Krista flatly. "She paid for tits with ass?"

Macie doubled over laughing. "Oh my God. You're hilarious," she said to Krista. Then the smile left as quickly as it had come. "But you didn't hear it from me, girls."

"Do you want to eat with us?" Krista asked.

"Well, that depends . . . ," said Macie.

"On what?" asked Kelly.

Macie reached into her bag and pulled out a Sharpie. "I

think we should let Leslie know what we think of sluts. Maybe on her locker, say, first thing in the morning?"

Krista looked at the Sharpie in Macie's outstretched hand, then looked up over her glasses with a grin.

"Atta girl," said Macie. "You've got potential, Kristen."

"It's Krista."

"Whatever. We'll see how you do tonight, and if it goes well, I'll work on names tomorrow at lunch."

"Macie! What are you doing?" I hissed as she pulled me away from the table.

On the other side of the vending machines, Macie stopped and burned holes through me with her eyes.

"I'm winning," she said softly. "It's what I do."

"But . . . Leslie didn't have a boob job—"

"How do you know?" said Beth. Macie and I both stopped and turned around. We'd forgotten she was following us.

I saw a slow smile spread across Macie's face as she cocked her head and looked once more at the tiny gymnast.

"Beth's exactly right, Jillian. Look around you. None of these students knows anything about us. Our whole class is a blank slate. The story gets written this week. The future of high school is set in the next four days. Get on board, or tell me now, and I'll find a new class vice president. Krista seems pretty resourceful, and Beth here is beginning to impress me."

The next morning, the word "WHORE" showed up in big, bold black letters scrawled across Leslie's locker, and

Leslie didn't show up for first period. When she walked into geometry second period, a general hush fell over the room. Then the talking started again, only this time in whispers. She saw me sitting in between Macie and Beth. She looked at me strangely, then settled into a desk across the room.

Krista walked up to our table at lunch and placed the Sharpie on Macie's tray. Macie saw the crimson fingernail polish and grabbed her wrist, which made Krista jump. Macie raised her eyes and winked.

"Where are you going? Sit."

Krista smirked and sat down with her lunch bag. "Thanks," she said.

"Nice work," said Macie. "Oh, and don't look now, but here comes Thunder Boobs."

"Didn't have to look," said Beth. "Felt the ground shaking."

Macie laughed so hard she almost spit out a mouthful of water. She was choking and coughing and pounding her chest as Leslie walked by, and just as she passed, Macie coughed the words, "Kill yourself."

Leslie wheeled on us. "What?" Her eyes were smoldering.

"Easy, Thunder Tits," said Macie. "Don't you need to go scrub your locker or something?"

Leslie smiled. "I'd love to chat, Macie, but Jake is waiting for me."

Macie narrowed her eyes as she watched Leslie go. "Not for long he's not."

• • •

"So our little Beth is no dummy. She decided to hitch her ride to the Macie Merrick bandwagon," Katherine said.

The phone was warm against my ear. I really wanted to hang up. Suddenly I was angry.

"Sort of the way you jumped on Macie's bandwagon?" I said. I was tired of Katherine's smugness, like she was somehow above all this.

"What are you talking about?"

"Oh, I don't know, Katherine." The sarcasm in my voice was thick, but I couldn't stop myself. "When I got back from summer vacation before junior year, suddenly I'd been replaced on the student council. What did she promise you?"

"This isn't about me and you anymore, Jillian. This is about all of us. I just think it's weird. Everybody says that Leslie and Beth seemed really close before school started, then Beth just ditched her?"

"Maybe you should ask Beth," I said.

Katherine sighed. "Okay. Look, Macie wants us to get together tomorrow night to discuss—just the girls. Is your place okay? After Beth gets done with practice around eight?"

Another call buzzed in, and I looked at the screen. It was Brad.

"Sure—that's fine. Sorry, Katherine—that's Brad. He's hopeless with calculus."

"Mm-hmm," she said. "You should probably get that. See you tomorrow."

I frowned as I clicked over. *What was that tone in her voice?*

"Hey," I said.

"I'm on my way over."

"What? Why?" I dropped my voice to a whisper, but I couldn't contain my grin. "Is Jake with you?" I asked.

"He will be," Brad said. "He's in the bathroom right now. We'll leave in five minutes. When you hear him come in, meet me on your sidewalk a few houses down. We have to talk."

"Brad? Is everything okay?"

"No," he said. "It's not."

I heard a door open behind him, and he hung up.

I climbed into Brad's truck four houses down from ours and he eased off the curb and turned around to head away from our windows.

"What is going on?" I asked.

Four blocks away from our street, he pulled to the end of a darkened cul-de-sac and switched off the lights.

"Who knows?" he asked quietly.

"About . . . what?"

"Us," he said.

"What?"

"Jake?" he asked.

"What about us—that we're . . . ?"

"Yes, Jillian!" he said, his voice raised. "Yes . . . that we're . . . whatever we are."

"No," I said. "Jesus, Brad. Why are you yelling?"

He reached over and grabbed his iPad off the seat of the truck and handed it to me. I looked at him.

"What?" I asked.

"Open it," he said.

I flipped open the magnetic cover and the screen blazed to life. I slid the lock off and entered his password—my birthday: 0723. The screen slid into place—an email shined into my eyes. There was no subject, and just a single line of text:

> The truth, the whole truth, and nothing but the truth.

I looked at Brad, confused. "What does this mean?"

"Scroll down." Brad put his forehead in his hand and leaned against the driver's-side window.

I flicked the email up with a swipe, and pictures flashed into view. A girl being kissed by a guy. In a car.

My car.

In the parking lot of a Starbucks.

It was us.

18. KATHERINE

On the way to Jillian's the next day, all I could hear in my head was Aunt Liza telling me not to show my cards, but I could feel the unrest in my stomach and I knew that if I didn't take deep breaths and stay calm, this whole thing could crack right down the middle like a cake on a cooling rack.

When I walked through the door, they were all looking at me. It was just the girls tonight.

"Did you ever find the video at your dad's office?" Macie snapped.

I didn't answer one way or another. "All I know is that Patrick said it was an unmitigated disaster."

No one was smiling. I'd been round and round in my head trying to figure out if I should show Macie the video of the deposition, but I just couldn't see what good it would do. We were already in this deep, and I didn't want to make this any worse on Beth than it was going to be.

"Why was it such a disaster?" Krista asked, looking from me to Beth and back again.

"The only reason it would have been a disaster is if somebody didn't deny everything the way we'd planned." Macie was on pins and needles. She was about to blow her stack, and for the first time in almost a year, I was ready to stand back and watch it happen.

Jillian reached over and patted Beth's hand. "I'm sure it wasn't that bad," she said. "What did he ask you about? What was he like?"

Beth glanced up at all of us from the couch I'd been sleeping on the morning we'd found out Leslie was dead less than two weeks ago. It felt like it had been a year. Suddenly I felt tired. Tired and old. As Aunt Liza called it, weary.

"He's handsome," said Beth. "He's got blue eyes and a nice smile . . ." Her voice trembled. She cleared her throat.

"Oh, who gives a shit what the lawyer is like?" blazed Macie. "They're all the fucking same. They want one thing. To trip us up. And it sounds like he succeeded."

"I'm sorry!" Beth yelled back, fighting tears. "It was awful. He brought up stuff that happened in ninth grade. He asked me if Leslie and I had been friends first."

"Friends," scoffed Macie, rolling her eyes. "I'll say."

"Shut up," Beth shot back. "Just. Shut. Up."

"Did you deny it?" Krista asked.

"I couldn't," Beth said, almost pleading. "I was under oath."

"Oh. My. God." Macie fell back against the couch across from Beth and closed her eyes, pinching the bridge of her nose with a thumb and forefinger like this was a bad dream and she could massage away the vision. "What else?" she asked, defeated.

"He asked me about the very first rumor. The one about the breast implants."

Macie didn't move a muscle, her hand still on her closed eyes. The room got very still as Krista and Jillian took in this news. They looked at Beth, and then at Macie. She musta felt the eyes all burrowing into her like a gopher in a bluegrass backyard 'cause her eyes popped open and she was on fire.

"What?" she spat. "What are you all looking at?"

Jillian and Beth both dropped their eyes, but not Krista. She glared at Macie, but turned to Beth. "What did you tell him about that rumor? Did you deny it?"

Beth kept her eyes trained on the shaggy blue area rug between the toes of her pink Chucks and shook her head.

"I told him I heard it. Then he wanted to know if I'd repeated it."

"And what did you say?" Macie asked in a tone that could have frozen the Mississippi in May.

Beth started crying. Hard. She covered her face with her hands. "I told him that he had no idea what it was like to be in high school—," she started.

"Great," Krista said flatly. "So basically you admitted that you were part of it."

"Fantastic," sneered Macie. "Way to go."

"Whatever, Macie." Beth was yelling now. "You're the one who started that rumor. This was all your idea in the first pla—"

Macie stood up, stopping Beth in midsentence, and took a very deliberate step around the coffee table between the couches. She slowly knelt down and looked into Beth's eyes.

"I swear to God, Beth. Don't you get it? If you don't start claiming not to know who started the rumors, we're all going down for this."

She stood back up and surveyed the rest of us like a mother mantis deciding whether to eat her husband now or later.

"So, how do they even know about all of this?" Krista asked. She was picking at the red polish on her nails, sending tiny flakes drifting into the carpet.

"It's their job to know," I said. "They've subpoenaed Facebook records, and between that and all the police interviews that were done last week with kids in the school, there's plenty to go on. They may even start to cooperate with Graham Braddock's office."

"What?" Macie asked, shocked.

"Who is Graham Braddock?" asked Jillian.

"The district attorney," I said quietly.

"They're working with the DA's office? On what? This is a civil suit," said Macie.

I took a deep breath. There was no way around this. "All I know is that Daddy said the DA is working with a couple of police detectives, continuing to take statements from students."

"That bastard . . ." Macie was grabbing her purse and fishing for her phone and her car keys.

"Why would the DA care about this?" Jillian was frowning, worried.

When I didn't answer right away, Macie looked up from her phone and rolled her eyes. "Go ahead, Katherine. Tell her. Clue them in, for fuck's sake."

"The DA would mainly be interested if there was going to be a criminal trial."

Macie's phone buzzed, and she glared at it, then tossed it into her bag. "There will be no criminal trial," she said. "My dad has enough dirt on Graham Braddock to bury him six feet deep. But let me assure you ladies that if we do not circle the wagons now, this will get far uglier before it gets better."

Just like that, camera-ready Macie was back in action, and I realized in that moment that I hated her. Truly, deeply hated her.

"Krista," she said. It was more a command than anything

else. When Krista looked at her, Macie said, "You and Josh are tomorrow after school, correct?"

"Yep," chirped Krista.

"I need you to stick with the plan," said Macie. "Deny it. Downplay it. Whatever they ask you about, just stay calm and tell them it didn't happen."

"You got it, boss." Krista smiled.

"Katherine?" The way she said my name made the back of my neck burn.I stared straight ahead. She waited for some confirmation that I'd heard her.

"Hello, Kat? You go on Monday, correct? Are you with me?" She snapped her fingers in front of my eyes like she was trying to bring me out of a hypnotized state.

"Don't call me 'Kat,'" I said slowly.

"Don't let me down," she said through clenched teeth. "Okay, Monday night after Katherine's deposition, let's meet to regroup at Pike Street, deal?"

Then she smiled and whirled toward the door. "And for chrissakes, cheer up, people! I mean, *really*, you guys. Nothing happened here. We weren't involved. Leslie Gatlin was a wing nut who killed herself because her parents weren't aware of her mental instability. Period. Unless one of you did something to Leslie on your own that I'm not aware of, you have nothing to worry about. I'll see you all tomorrow. Remember to be there early—it's TeenReach volunteer sign-up day. I'll need all four of you to help me man the table."

Then she blew us a kiss like we'd been discussing pom-poms and push-up bras, and disappeared into the hallway.

Aunt Liza called when I was on my way home from Jillian's. It'd been a coupla weeks since we'd talked. I almost didn't answer when I saw her on the caller ID. I wasn't sure what to say. I wasn't sure how to tell her. I wasn't sure how to ask for help. I wasn't sure that I needed help, but I pushed the button on the steering wheel that answers my phone hands-free anyhow, 'cause I was sure I needed to hear her voice.

"Hey, Aunt Liza."

"Hey, Li'l K."

And something about hearing her voice broke me open just a little on the inside and I choked out a sob that musta sounded like a hydrogen bomb in a blender, so I gripped that steering wheel and told her the whole story about what was going on in Seattle.

When I'd finished, Aunt Liza was real quiet. It had started to rain lightly, and I turned on the windshield wipers. They made a slow, smooth *swoosh* across the windshield.

"Li'l K, you remember when you first wanted to do pageants?"

"Yes, ma'am," I said. "After that night you and I watched Miss America on TV while Mama and Daddy were in New Orleans for the weekend."

"Mmm-hmm," she said. "And you remember what we watched the next night?"

"*My Fair Lady*," I said with a smile.

Aunt Liza laughed in the way she does. "That Audrey Hepburn was more'n just a pretty face," she said. "She had brains like you, too. In fact, you're more like her than you'll ever know. But, Li'l K, when you go into that room and you sit there with those lawyers, you got to tell the truth. Even if you afraid. Fear is what got you into this mess—fear of what other people think, fear you ain't beautiful enough as you is, fear that if you stand up, you'll be all alone."

I was crying again.

"You was too young to remember this when we watched the movie together, but that Miz Hepburn always been one of my favorites 'cause a something she said 'fore she died. I wrote it down when I heard it years and years ago. Keep it in my dresser drawer with my favorite things."

"What was it?" I asked.

"It was her instructions for bein' beautiful," Aunt Liza said.

"What were they?"

I heard her clear her throat and I pictured her there in Atlanta, talking into the phone with her eyes closed, remembering.

"For beautiful eyes, look for the good in others; for beautiful lips, speak only words of kindness; and for poise, walk with the knowledge that you are never alone."

It's funny how a lifetime of people talking at you can make you numb to hearing your own voice, but somehow the right person can say the right thing in the right moment—even if it's something they've said before, or something you've heard before—and when it rat-a-tats across your eardrum, for some reason at that precise second, you hear it. You hear it loud and clear, like a heavenly bullhorn, or the beat of the bass in a song you've always loved.

Aunt Liza cut through the haze of all the other voices I'd been hearing in my ears and my head, and suddenly, in the silence, I heard the voice in my heart.

I pressed down on the gas and finally felt ready for my deposition. I knew exactly what I had to do.

19. BETH

When I got home from Jillian's, Mom's Bible study was just finishing up. There were still seven or eight women hanging out, drinking coffee and eating cake and cookies. I'd almost made it through the living room when I heard my mom's voice.

"Oh, Bethany, honey. How wonderful you're home! How did things go at your deposition? Mrs. Warren, Bethany has been called as a witness in a civil case! It's very important! Did you say hello to Mrs. Warren, Bethany?"

I stopped, then slowly turned. "No, Mom, actually I was fleeing through the living room in hopes of not being noticed. I'm tiny and fast." I smiled to Mrs. Warren, who must've been eighty if she was a day. "Usually I can get away with it."

Mrs. Warren blinked at me, then said, "My grandson Stanley is at the Christian school down by the airport. He's a junior there. Plays basketball. Bet you all would have a lot in common." She smiled.

"I'll bet we would," I said. "Especially calculus homework. Nice seeing you, Mrs. Warren."

"Bethany . . . ," Mom said. "I wish you could stay for a moment—"

"That makes one of us." I smiled sweetly and waved as I rounded the bend with my bag and headed upstairs.

I opened my laptop and logged on to Gmail. The first message was from Coach Stevens with the details for the meet next weekend. The second email was from an address I didn't recognize, but the subject said, "Regarding Leslie." I clicked it and froze.

Inside the email was a screenshot of Leslie's Facebook page from the morning she died. There was the message she'd left for me on her wall:

> List Chick, I'm sorry I didn't feel the same way about you. I could've been your friend. Anchors away.

Underneath the screenshot in bold black letters were the words: *You're only as sick as your secrets.*

A wave of nausea swept over me and I ran into the bathroom just in time. I wanted to cry, but there were no tears, just fear. I was sweating and freezing at the same time. A cold sweat broke out on my forehead as I wiped my mouth and flushed the toilet. I used some mouthwash, then raced back into my room and locked the door.

I looked back down at the screen and noticed a Gchat window blinking with the message: "hipstermatic94 has invited you to chat." It was the same address the email was from.

listchick1: who is this?

hipstermatic94: Let's not play games okay?

listchick1: FUCK YOU KRISTA

listchick1: WHY ARE YOU DOING THIS TO ME?

hipstermatic94: You better come see me if you want to find out. We should talk.

listchick1: I can't. I have homework to do.

hipstermatic94: We all do. So you should come talk now so we can get back to Calculus.

hipstermatic94: Or you can just find out how it goes down in my deposition tomorrow.

listchick1: You are such a bitch.

hipstermatic94: See you soon . . .

I slammed closed my computer, grabbed my keys, and drove to Krista's.

Krista's little brother Sam buzzed me in at their loft when I knocked. He was wearing a SPAM T-shirt and holding a hot glue gun.

"Hey," he said. "Krista's in her room."

"Thanks," I said, and pushed past him. When I got to the top of the stairs, I paused and looked at the light coming out from under Krista's door. My hand was shaking. I grasped the top of the banister to steady it. I couldn't tell if I was furious or terrified. I settled on both and walked down the hall as silently as possible.

"Oh—totally." Krista's goose honk laugh was coming through the cracked door. "I swear to God she's shaking like a leaf."

I reached out to push open the door, but a second voice stopped me.

"It's so genius that you took that screenshot."

It was Macie.

"She was so upset that morning that I wasn't sure she saw it, but the minute she got in the shower, I nabbed a screen grab and sent it to myself," said Krista. "That's when I knew for sure."

Three years of frustration broke loose somewhere near my right hamstring, and the next thing I knew, I raised my right foot in a kung fu kick and the door flew open, breaking the mirror on the back.

Krista shrieked and Macie jumped.

"Knew what for sure?" I yelled as I advanced on Krista, who was sitting on the floor in front of her bed. I was on my knees and grabbed her by the collar of her jean jacket. I pinned her against the bed and shook her once, good and hard.

Macie started to laugh. "Oh, Beth. You're so cute. Here, put Krista down."

She pried my hands off Krista, who was scrambling for her glasses, which had been knocked off when I pushed her up against the bed. Just as she reached for them, I slammed my foot down on them, feeling the vintage plastic crack beneath my foot.

"You bitch," Krista yelled.

Sam appeared at the door, holding an ice cream sandwich.

"Sam! Get out of here. Go to your own room," Krista commanded.

"Just wanted to let you know that Mom called a minute ago. She's on her way home from her shift at the hospital," he said, then looked at Krista's glasses, and noticed the shards of mirror lying on the area rug and the dark wood floor. "Everything okay?"

"Just working some things out," said Macie brightly.

Sam slowly turned around and walked toward the stairs. Macie reached over and closed the door.

"Let's make this brief, Beth. Due to your epic meltdown this week, the rest of us are in deep shit. You copped to the rumor about the boobs, which throws Krista under the bus for writing 'whore' on Leslie's locker."

"This is all bullshit," I said. "You've lied so much for so long you don't know what the truth is anymore."

"I know the truth about one thing," sneered Krista. "They're going to jump all over me for the Sharpie-on-the-locker thing, and they'll rake Josh over the coals for his stunt. But they're missing some of the more colorful history about our little group."

My stomach jumped into my throat. "What history?" I asked.

"Here, let me read some of it to you." Krista picked up a worn lavender envelope and took out a piece of stationery that was inside. She opened it and read:

Dear Beth—

I've never told anyone that you tried to kiss me. I don't know why you hate me so much. Ever since that day in my garage, you won't even look me in the eye. I told you then, and I'll say it again now: I don't care if you're gay. I didn't ever want to hurt you. I just wanted you to be my friend.

Can we try to be friends again? Can you try to get Macie and the other girls to stop being so mean to me? I don't know how much more of this I can take. I'm tired of crying every day. I'm tired of feeling worthless.

I want you to have this necklace. It reminds me of those two weeks before freshman year when I thought you were going to be my best friend. Maybe it will remind you of those good times too.

Love, Leslie

When Krista finished reading, she slipped the note back into the envelope and smiled at me.

"Where did you get that?" I was shaking. The room was spinning.

"Don't you remember?" Macie said with wide eyes. "Leslie tried to give it to you at your birthday party, but you refused to take it."

It all came rushing back in a flood. Leslie showing up at my party the week before she died. The argument in the driveway. Begging her to leave.

"Probably didn't want anything to do with the girl who turned you down, huh?" Krista smirked.

"I always thought you were a little lesbo." Macie giggled. "I mean, you're little choppy pixie cut is so dykadelish. When sharp-eyed Krista here retrieved this envelope from your mailbox after your birthday, that confirmed my suspicions."

"Then, lo and behold, a wall post the morning Leslie died. It was the last wall post she made. Her official final Facebook act," said Macie.

"Must make you feel pretty special, eh, List Chick One?" Krista sneered.

When my hand flew at Krista's face, Macie stopped my wrist and said in a low voice, "Thought that was you."

I dropped to my knees crying.

"We're going to share equal portions of this thing, Beth. Just wanted you to know that the secret is about to be out. Krista's going in tomorrow and telling them what we all know."

"And what do you know?" I sobbed.

"That you were in love with Leslie. You turned on her because she didn't want to be with you."

"All you've got is a necklace and a letter," I choked out. "That's not enough to pin all of this on me. They'll never buy that."

"Maybe they won't," said Krista. "But your Mom's Bible study sure will."

"And my dad's press secretary." Macie smiled. "Besides, the thing the lawyers will believe is that you set up the fake Facebook account that we used to send Leslie a weekly message."

Krista snickered. "Yeah, they'll believe that because it's true. In fact, pretty much all the bullying that's gone on in the last year can be linked to an account set up by your IP address. We know the lawyers have already subpoenaed the records from Facebook. I'll bet they've read every message you sent Leslie Gatlin in your account and the fake account, and that'll be enough evidence to stop this conversation once and for all."

"If I were you, Beth, I'd come clean," said Macie flatly. "If anyone should cop to Leslie Gatlin's death, it's you."

"I can see it now," said Krista. "'Spurned High School Lesbian Drives Girl Crush to Suicide.'"

I stood up and wiped my nose with the back of my hand. "You two will never get away with this," I said softly.

Macie laughed. "Oh dear, sweet Beth. We already have."

20. JAKE

The upstairs bathroom in our house separates my bedroom from Jillian's. We've both got a door and a sink. She usually uses the tub, I use the shower. It basically blows having to share. It just always takes her forever to get ready, and I know that sounds like a totally sexist comment, but I just don't understand how somebody can take two hours to get dressed for a football game. It's also jacked when I don't wanna see her or talk to her, like tonight.

But there she was.

Washing her face.

And now it was too late, 'cause she'd seen me and she had soap in her eyes and she was trying to rinse and find the hand towel and turn off the water all at once, and frankly, it was funny, but I didn't feel much like laughing.

As I turned to go, it was like she sensed the action in my

legs, because in the split second it took for my brain to send my legs the signal, I heard her through the towel she was blotting across her face:

"Jake. *Wait!*"

And something in me froze. It was the desperation in her voice. The pleading in the word "wait." It stopped me in the doorway that led to my room.

"Jake, you can't just stop talking to me," she said. She tossed the towel onto the sink counter. I stood there silently, watching her squirm.

Who are you?

I looked for some signal of recognition. Some flicker of the four-year-old girl with the pigtails who I used to protect when Kevin, Kathy, and Kyle, the triplets we lived next door to at the time, tried to coax her away from her Big Wheel. Kevin and Kyle would try to distract her, and then that little bitch Kathy would jump on her Big Wheel and cruise down the sidewalk. I'd take on both of Kathy's brothers at once. I was ferocious when it came to Jillian.

I looked at her closely. Same reddish-brown hair; same light freckles across her nose, uncovered from the layer of powder that carefully blots them out each morning. The same eyes sparkled in the new halogen pin spots I'd helped Dad install after we moved in and remodeled the upstairs.

"See?" she said. "You're doing it again. Just standing there pouting. You can't even look me in the eye."

That's it.

It took two slo-mo steps to cross the bathroom. Jillian backed up into the doorjamb by her sink, her back pressed against the towel bar. I bent down so my nose was inches from hers, and stared directly into her eyes.

"Do you have something to say, Jillian?" I whispered. "'Cause I'm all ears."

She stood there, shocked and scared, but not flinching. Her eyes flooded and she blinked but didn't look away. Then she surprised me and threw her arms around me. I felt her bury her face in the space between my shoulder and my neck. I felt the heat of her tears on my shirt.

"Jake," she choked into my neck, and then a single word: "Please."

As I held her there in the bathroom and listened to her sob, something in me melted just enough to stay in the room.

After her sobs subsided, I pulled back from her and said, "Walk me through this, Jills, 'cause I just don't understand it."

"That's just it, Jake," she said. "There's nothing to walk through. I keep feeling like you want me to explain how this isn't my fault, but I shouldn't have to."

I let this sink in, and then said, "Still listening."

"Jake." She put both hands on my shoulders. "Not everybody fits in. Not everybody can be friends all the time. That doesn't mean I wanted Leslie to die. None of us did. I know you're sad, but, Jake, you know Leslie's parents are a crapshoot at best. She was probably more unstable than any of us realized. I mean, look at her dad—he's a nutcase, and her mom is a drunk. Mental illness obviously runs in that family."

"Jillian, this is not about anyone's mental illness except Macie Merrick's," I said softly.

"Jesus, Jake." She rolled her eyes and shook her head. "Macie is not the problem here."

The melted part of me became an explosion. "Goddammit, Jillian! How long are you going to keep saying that? You're going to cling to that leaky plank like it's a life raft no matter how huge the tsunami of evidence is, aren't you?"

"Jake! Listen!" She was crying.

"No, Jillian. I've heard enough. I don't know what fucking power Macie Merrick holds over all of you, but she never held it over me. Never. I am so sick of hearing you all make excuses for her bullshit. You, Brad, Katherine, everybody."

Jillian slumped against the counter, then exploded back toward me. "Stop it. Stop it!"

"I can't believe you," I said. "Stop it? Stop telling you how horrible Macie is for you? If you were about to drink a glass of poison, I'd yell and scream and tell you exactly what was going on. I can't wait to get you in front of those lawyers and lay out the shit you guys pulled with Leslie one day at a time for the last three years. I can't wait to watch you squirm."

"What are you talking about?" Jillian's voice shook in a register so low I could barely hear her.

"Didn't Mom tell you about our deposition?"

"She told me about *my* deposition," she said. "When's yours?"

"At the same time, Jillian. They want to question us together because we're brother and sister."

Jillian was finally quiet. "What does that have to do with anything?"

"Beats me," I said. "But if you so much as look like you might blink in a way that would mislead these lawyers, I will nail you to the wall."

Jillian started sobbing again. "You don't have any idea what it's like for the girls in your life. You and Brad don't have to play the game because you're both good-looking and athletes. You've never been bad at anything in your life but Spanish sophomore year."

"I'm done here," I said.

"Well, I'm *not done*!" she yelled at me. "You think it's just as easy for everybody else as it is for you. Well, it isn't, and you don't take two seconds to notice that. You've never had to defend yourself. I almost lost Macie last year when Katherine came along." She held up her thumb and forefinger an inch apart. "I am *this close* to being done with high school, and I am not letting things fall apart."

Jillian was crying so hard when she fell to her hands and knees by the tub that I was afraid she might be sick. Something about her sitting there on the floor, crying, made a knot form in my chest. I felt like I was being pulled in two. I thought about us talking to each other in words no one could understand so many years ago. All this time, it had been me and her. That felt like it was falling apart now, too. I stood there watching her cry for what seemed like a very long time. Then, slowly, I knelt down by her and put my hand on her back.

"Jillian?" I said softly. "What is it? Tell me how we can keep it from falling apart."

"I want to tell you, so bad, Jake, but I . . . I just . . ."

"Jillian, this is your chance," I whispered. "Tell me now. If it comes out in the deposition, it'll be worse because it'll be evidence. If you tell me now, we can fix it."

"It's . . ." Jillian searched my eyes and took a deep breath, then dropped her gaze to the floor. "It's Brad."

"What about Brad?" I asked.

"We've been . . . we're . . ."

"What, Jillian?"

"Together."

I sat down next to her, my back against the cabinets under the sink. "You mean . . . like . . . dating?"

"Something . . . ," she said. "I mean, he's dating Macie, but . . . somebody knows."

"How?" I asked.

"They emailed pictures of us kissing to Brad."

"Oh . . . wow." I started to laugh. "Brad?" I giggled. "Bradley Wyst?"

"Shut up." Jillian slapped me on the leg. I rolled over onto my back on the floor and laughed harder.

"Jake! It's not funny!"

"Kinda," I gasped. "Kinda it is funny."

"What am I gonna do?" Jillian was beside herself. "If Macie finds out, I'm dead."

"Jills, don't be so dramatic," I said. "Obviously one of the girls sent you those pics."

"How can you be so sure?" she asked.

"Because nobody else gives a damn," I said.

"Well, Macie will give a damn."

"Don't you get it yet? She was probably the one who sent them to you."

Jillian wiped her cheeks. I stood and offered her my hand. Slowly she placed hers in mine, and I pulled her up.

"Jills?"

"Yeah?"

"Is that all?" I asked. "Is that *everything*?"

"Yes," she said. "That's everything."

Maybe it was her tears. Or maybe a part of me really wanted my sister back. Maybe I'm just a moron.

Whatever the reason, I swear I believed her.

21. JILLIAN

By seven thirty a.m. we were all in our places behind the Teen-Reach volunteer table. Beth sat down between me and Katherine. No one spoke; we just sat behind our clipboards, waiting. Macie buzzed about in a short silver suit with a spangled top and her signature Jimmy Choo heels. She looked like she was ready to go live from the scene of the crime as soon as the cameras showed up. She had just finished hanging the banner on the wall behind us when Krista rounded the corner. Her glasses were missing, and she had a cardboard travel tray of coffee.

"Morning!" she said brightly, passing out Starbucks for everyone. "I got you tea, Beth," she said softly. "You like chamomile, right?"

Beth looked up and took the cup from her. I watched her nostrils flare, and something passed between them besides the Venti paper cup.

Slowly, over the next twenty minutes, the hallway filled up. The early swim practice was first to hit the stairs, most of them racing by us to ditch their gear in their lockers and head across the street to McDonald's to scarf down as many calories as they could before the first bell rang.

"Skinny bitches," muttered Beth.

When I smiled, Beth caught my eye and smiled back. "I remember carbs," I said.

"Oh, please, Jillian, you're five eleven. You can eat nothing but lard and hamburger buns and never worry. I've got to spray-glue my leotard to my ass as it is."

"Better than your tits in your gown." Katherine laughed.

"Oh, that's right!" said Macie. "When is Miss Washington Teen?"

"I don't expect any of y'all to be there." Katherine looked down at the empty clipboard in front of her. We'd been sitting here for thirty minutes and no one had stopped yet.

"Don't be ridiculous. Missing you winning the regional was bad enough." Beth rolled her eyes. "Of course I'm coming. You in, Jillian?"

"It's Saturday night," Katherine said.

"Awesome," said Macie. "These depositions will be almost over by then. Who knows? Maybe they'll even withdraw the suit by then and this thing will be put to rest. Either way, let's all go and celebrate."

"What we celebrating, ladies?" It was Josh. He was carrying a McDonald's bag and holding a Sausage McMuffin.

"Wow," I said. "How many of those do you eat after practice?"

"Usually only two, but I didn't have time for the full pancake breakfast this morning, so I'm having three."

"Bastard," Beth yelled with a smile, and threw a pen at his head.

"Have to keep my girlish figure." He winked. "Wow, you guys have quite the operation going here," he said. "Nice banner."

"Yeah, turned out pretty well," Macie said. "The Teen-Reach people were really jazzed about combining their logo with Westport's. Let's take a picture, everybody!"

Macie reached into her bag and pulled out her phone, then handed it to Josh. "You mind doing the honors?"

"Not at all," he said.

Josh stepped across the hall and we all leaned together. "Oh, c'mon, ladies. This looks like a funeral. Smile a little, would ya?"

He snapped a couple of pictures, then grabbed his own phone. "One more!" he said.

As he handed Macie's phone back to her and resumed stuffing McMuffin in his face, he looked at the sign-up lists.

"Not a lot of volunteer action, huh?"

"Nope," said Beth.

"Interesting," said Josh.

I saw Macie's eyes narrow. She's like a robot when it comes to reading people. "What's interesting about that, Josh?" Suddenly her voice had the timbre of a glacier.

Josh's eyes met Macie's as he took a bite of his McMuffin. He chewed slowly, holding her gaze. "Just sayin'."

"Ready for your deposition today?" she asked.

It wasn't a question. It was a challenge.

Josh chewed slowly, considering her. Finally he swallowed and chased the bite with a swig from a plastic bottle of OJ hidden in the bag.

"I don't think that's the question you should be asking," Josh said with a smile sweeter than Splenda. "Are *you* ready for my deposition, Macie?"

He said it like he was joking, but it was sly, and Macie caught it. She blinked at him, and I saw color rise in her cheeks.

"You know the reason nobody is signing up, right?" he asked her, nodding at the banner. She was quiet. "It's because they want to see how this all turns out. Hanging out with Macie Merrick isn't enough to fill a clipboard with volunteers the way it used to be." He smirked, then slowly, without moving his eyes away from Macie, he crumpled up a McMuffin wrapper and held it in a clenched fist.

"Careful, Josh." Macie smiled with everything but her eyes. "Wouldn't want to air your dirty laundry in public, would we?"

Josh tossed his head back and laughed. His dark-brown

hair was still wet from the pool, and you could see his abs through his polo. Three years of swimming had been good to him. "That's my girl," he said to Macie. Then in a mock "Eureka!" moment, he slapped his hand to his forehead, his eyes wide. "Oh. Em. Gee! You should totally meet my girlfriend sometime. You two have a lot in common."

Macie didn't take the bait, but Beth did. "I didn't know you had a girlfriend!" She giggled. "What's her name?"

"Elaine Braddock." Josh smiled at her. "She's a freshman at Stanford, pre-law. She's flying up for my meet next weekend. You should come."

"Wait, Braddock—like, District Attorney Graham Braddock?" I asked.

"That's her dad," Josh exclaimed more cheerfully than required. "The DA invited me over for dinner tonight. He and his wife want me to help plan a surprise party for Elaine next weekend. They want to help me prep for my deposition tomorrow, too."

He turned and smiled at Macie. "You should all totally come to the party! I'll send you the Facebook invite. Just remember, Macie, it's a secret."

He leaned in to Macie and held a finger to his lips. "Ssssshhhhh . . ." He tossed his McDonald's sack into the trash can next to the table and winked at her. "Good luck with the sign-ups." Then he held up two fingers to the rest of us as he headed down the hall. "Peace, ladies."

I looked back at Macie. She was gripping the back of an empty folding chair so hard that her knuckles were turning white. In something between a twitch and a spasm, she pushed it violently into the table, making everybody jump.

"Sorry," she said, taking out her phone and dialing a number. "I'll be right back."

Macie grabbed her bag and in long, angry strides, walked to the bathrooms across the hall and pushed open the door to the ladies' room. Krista started to stand up, but I beat her around the end of the table.

"Give us a minute," I said. Krista frowned as she slumped back down in her chair.

When I pushed into the bathroom, Macie was wrapping up her call.

"Who was that?" I asked.

"Just giving my dad's press secretary the heads-up about Josh. She's making a couple of calls."

Slowly, Macie grasped both sides of a sink and let her head hang loose, her eyes closed. I stood and watched her, not sure what to say. Finally she turned her head toward me. Her eyes were glassy. She was looking at me, but she wasn't seeing me.

"When my dad was running for senate and Marty went through all that shit, I swore to God that I would never be the reason my dad lost anything," she said softly.

I walked over to her and gently put my hand next to hers on the sink so that our pinkies touched.

"I know," I said. "I was there. Remember?"

Macie's eyes focused on me then, and she saw me. Really saw me. And this is that thing that I couldn't explain to Jake last night in the bathroom: what it feels like when Macie Merrick sees you, really sees you. There is this thing that she has—her dad has it too. It spills out of her eyes and floods you with this feeling that you're the only one who matters, that what happens next is of no consequence, because right now, you've captured her attention and this is the only moment that matters.

The simple truth was that I felt better when I was in Macie Merrick's gaze. In the moment that her eyes locked with mine, the knowledge that I was a prettier, smarter, funnier person was never up for debate. If I could see that Macie believed I was good enough, then I swore it must've been true.

Somehow knowing that Macie didn't doubt me made me not doubt myself. She gave me permission to actually believe the things I'd like to think about myself. And if I believed those things about myself—even for a moment—then who was to say they weren't true?

Macie smiled at me and locked my pinkie with hers, our hands still on the sink. "Thanks, Jills."

I watched in the mirror as she went into a stall, then I splashed some water on my face. As I was blotting dry with a paper towel, I saw the door swing open and Kelly, the redhead from the volleyball team, came in and fished in her purse for a lipstick. She saw me standing at the sink and looked away without smiling. As she touched the lipstick to her mouth, Macie came out of the stall and walked to the sink next to Kelly's to wash her hands.

Kelly froze for a moment and stared at Macie for just a second too long.

"I think the Gay-Straight Alliance meetings are in the bathrooms upstairs," Macie said coldly. "Maybe you could quit staring and get the hell out of here?"

I have witnessed Macie Merrick clear entire classrooms with a comment like this. As warm as her charm can be, there is a ruthless streak inside her that could laser through reinforced concrete. I tossed my paper towel into the trash can and waited for Kelly to turn and flee.

But something else happened instead.

Kelly kept staring directly into Macie's eyes in the mirror and slowly finished applying her lipstick. Then she smacked her lips once and smiled at Macie.

"Seem a little stressed out, Macie. Things not going so well with the Gatlin case?"

Macie's eyes narrowed. "What would you know about that?"

Kelly dropped her lipstick into her purse and grabbed a paper towel to blot. When she'd finished, she turned to Macie.

"You pretend that you don't remember me in the hallways, but I know you do. I was the girl sitting next to Krista on the first day of freshman year when you started that rumor about Leslie and the plastic surgeon. I was so afraid of you that day that I stopped talking to Leslie. In fact, I was one of the people who should have been her friend, but I was a coward. I knew you were lying, but I didn't want you to start a lie about me—"

"Sorry," Macie interrupted her. "I'm bored now. Jillian? Shall we?"

As Macie walked toward the door, Kelly shook her head and laughed. "You know why no one is signing up at your little table out there, right?"

Macie turned on her heel and marched right back to Kelly, dropping her bag off her shoulder and onto the floor. Kelly flinched and stepped backward.

"Please," said Macie coolly. "Enlighten us."

Two freshmen girls walked into the bathroom. Macie fixed them with her camera-ready high-beam smile. "Girls, so glad you could join us for a new first-period drama class here in the first-floor women's restroom. A former friend of the late Leslie Gatlin's was just about to share with us why no one is signing up to volunteer at the TeenReach Hotline."

She turned back to Kelly. "You were saying?"

The freshmen stood frozen and wide-eyed, stuck somewhere between fight and flight. Kelly dropped all pretense. She stared at Macie solemnly and shook her head.

"I pity you, Macie. The only thing more tragic than watching you rise to power has been watching it unravel."

"Ha! Oh my God." Macie tossed her head back in a staccato laugh. "You? Pity me? That's rich," she said bitterly.

"You'll get away with this," Kelly continued. "You'll beat the civil suit, and your dad will keep everything hush-hush, and you'll probably still get into Harvard or Yale, or Brown, or wherever, and you'll move on to a new group of minions who have no idea that you're this vicious, brutal person who always comes out on top by crushing the people in your way."

The air was so still I realized I was holding my breath.

"That's not who I am." Macie spoke slowly, barely containing her rage.

"Keep believing that, Macie," Kelly said. "Just know that there are people in this school who finally get it now. There are a few of us who see exactly who you are and exactly what you do." Kelly shifted her bag to her right shoulder and walked past Macie toward the door. She turned and stopped as she reached for the handle.

"I don't care what your lawyers or your parents or the press or the principal say, Macie. You might as well have blown a hole in Leslie Gatlin with a gun. Sure, she took her own life, and that's on her. I abandoned her back in ninth grade, and that's on me. But most of it? It's on you, Macie."

The freshman girls wisely followed Kelly out of the bathroom without making a sound.

Macie dropped her bag onto the counter at the sink and dug out some mascara. She pulled out the brush and held it to her left upper lid. I watched as it shook for a moment in front of the mirror. She closed her eyes, took a deep breath, and then opened them again. She brought the brush up once more and, with a steady hand, applied a fresh layer.

As we turned to leave, I heard her phone ding, and Macie paused to pull it out of her purse. She read the message and smiled, then dropped her phone back into her bag.

"What was that?" I asked.

"The end of Josh Phillips," she said.

She threw back her shoulders and held the bathroom door open for me with a big smile."Shall we?"

Macie wove her arm through mine, and together we walked out of the bathroom and through the path that cleared for us in the hallway.

Later that day, on my way to fourth period, I got a text from Brad.

`Lunch? Bleachers?`

I typed back *yep* and smiled to myself. I could tell he'd been tense about the pictures, but it made me nervous when he didn't call or text.

He was waiting for me on the last set of bleachers at the opposite end of the field from the cafeteria windows. When he saw me coming, he ran his hand through his hair and smiled, like he was bashful, or nervous. My heart flipped a little.

He's so cute when he does that.

"Hey," he said.

I walked up to him and stood on my tiptoes to kiss him, but he stepped backward. "Whoa, Jills. Hang on."

"What?" I asked.

He just looked at me. And in that moment I knew. *This is what it looks like when things fall apart.*

I reached out toward him again. "No," I said, louder than I meant to. "Brad?" My voice sounded panicked and desperate.

"I can't, Jills."

"No!" Angry tears brimmed over and flooded my cheeks. It was an ugly cry.

"Jillian, I'm so sorry, but if Macie finds out, I'll lose my internship. You know that I don't have the brains you and Jake do."

"What internship?" I was shouting now. I didn't understand. All I wanted was for him to wrap his arms around me.

Instead, he hung his head and dug the toe of his high-top into the ground. He squinted off to the side, like he was looking for something over the roof of the music building.

"Jillian, Macie's dad is going to give me an internship at his office this summer in order to make up for the D-minus I got in US Government last year. Jenkins has signed off on it. If I complete the internship, I'll finish with a three-point-oh GPA, which is enough to qualify for a scholarship to USC with Jake."

"So . . . that's it? Your *grades* are suddenly more important to you than I am?"

"Jills, that's not fair."

"Except that my dad can't give you an internship, I guess?"

His chin dropped to his chest as he stared at the grass between his high-tops.

"Brad, we don't even know where the pictures came from."

"I can't risk it, Jillian. You know how Macie gets."

"Yeah," I said quietly. "I do know. Which is why you should be with *me*."

I turned around and walked back toward the cafeteria. I pulled out my phone and texted my mom: *Really sick. Heading home. Will you call the office?*

I kept walking past the cafeteria patio and got into my car in the back parking lot. As I turned the key in the ignition, my phone buzzed and jumped on the passenger seat. Macie had texted me a picture of Brad and me in front of the bleachers, which she must've taken from the third floor of the music building. After the picture came a second text:

`Did you really think I didn't know? Don't cross me. In your deposition keep our secret a secret.`

22. KATHERINE

As I stepped away from the window in the music building, Macie turned and smiled.

"That should keep things with Jillian in check," she said like she was crossin' "milk" and "eggs" off of a grocery list. "Thank you, Katherine, for the pictures and . . . your help on this."

I nodded and smiled. "Anytime," I said.

"You put the 'vice' in 'vice president.'" She giggled. "Coming?" she asked as she almost skipped into the hall, and held the door of the practice room open for me.

"Right behind you," I said.

"Don't be late for Brit lit," she said. "We're getting our research paper assignments. You don't want to get stuck with Elizabeth Barrett Browning again."

After she left, I slumped down onto the piano bench and

leaned my head back against the carpet squares that covered the wall behind me for soundproofing. I checked the time on my phone. I had ten minutes before lunch was over and class started.

I dialed Jillian's number. When the call went to voice mail, I left a message:

"Hi, Jillian. It's Katherine. Look, I need to talk to you and Beth tonight. Text me whenever and let me know what time works for you."

I left the same message for Beth, then I left the practice room, and the music building, and the school. I drove to my dad's office, and when I couldn't find him or his secretary, I wandered down the hall to Patrick's office. Liz greeted me with a wave and a smile. She clicked the mouse on her computer and pulled her earbuds out.

"Hey, Katherine." She smiled. "Out of school early?"

"Something like that." I smiled. "Do you know where my dad is?"

"Big company meeting today. The brass has everybody on a conference call talking about whatever it is they talk about. They always keep me out here to man the phones—which suits me. The Atlanta folks are the only ones who ever call here, anyway, so with everyone on the same line, it gets pretty quiet."

I stayed at Daddy's office and did homework all afternoon. At one point, I fell asleep on his couch and woke up with little bumps on my face from the fabric of the throw pillows. Looked like I'd fallen asleep on a waffle iron.

Eventually, he came in and we talked about the brief he was working on—an unclear deed of ownership, disputed by the great-aunt of the previous owner, or something like that. He was in the middle of talking to me about it when Patrick walked down the hall from the conference room with the camera.

"Hey, Katherine." Patrick smiled. "You ready for tomorrow?"

"As I'll ever be, I suppose." I smiled.

"Good luck this weekend," he said, then turned to my dad. "Daysun, here are the latest depositions."

Daddy knew exactly what I wanted. He handed me the camera. "You wanna do the honors, young lady?"

I smiled and plugged the camera into my laptop and started the download.

"I don't understand why you want us to see this," grumbled Beth.

She was sitting cross-legged on Jillian's bed with her arms folded across her chest, scowling.

Jillian was quiet. She seemed preoccupied.

"Is everything okay?" I asked her.

"I'm fine," she said. Not annoyed or impatient, just . . . flatline. "What are we watching again?"

"I've got Josh's and Krista's depositions."

Beth's eyes went wide as her chin dropped. "But you told Macie that you couldn't get them."

I sighed. "I don't tell her everything."

This time, Jillian's eyes were wide. Slowly she looked at Beth, then back at me. I clicked play.

"Please state your name for the record." Kellan Dirkson was all business.

"Joshua Franklin Phillips."

Lauren Wolinsky leaned into frame. "Raise your right hand and repeat after me."

I pushed fast-forward.

"Wait—what's he saying?" asked Jillian.

"These are just standard questions, identification of Leslie Gatlin, establishing length of his relationship with her, the nature of the relationship. . . . Here we go." I hit play.

"Did you ever message Leslie Gatlin from your personal Facebook account?"

"No," Josh replied.

"Did you ever message Leslie Gatlin from someone else's Facebook account?"

"No."

"Have you ever established a secondary Facebook account under an assumed name?"

"Yes," said Josh. His voice was crisp and clear. There was no hesitation.

"What was the name on this account?" Kellan asked.

"Craig Hutchins," he said.

Jillian gasped. "Oh my God. He's actually going to tell them."

"Shh!" Beth leaned in closer to the laptop, eyes aglow. "Turn it up!"

"What kind of messages did you send from this account under the name of Craig Hutchins?" Kellan Dirkson already seemed to know this information. I was sure he'd subpoenaed every Facebook account Leslie had ever received a message from.

"Mainly, I sent messages to Leslie Gatlin," said Josh, cool as a cucumber. No sweating, no flinching—nothing. "I sent her messages telling her how attractive she was and asking her to meet me for a date."

"As Craig Hutchins?" asked Kellan Dirkson.

"Yes," answered Josh.

"Why wouldn't you just ask Leslie Gatlin out on a date as yourself?" Kellan asked.

A slow grin spread across Josh's face. "Well, mainly because she's not my type. I date college girls. And cougars."

Kellan sighed. "Then why ask her out as a nonexistent person?"

"Macie Merrick wanted me to."

"Macie Merrick asked you to send falsified Facebook messages to Leslie Gatlin?" asked Kellan.

"Yes," said Josh.

"And did Miss Gatlin respond to the messages in turn?" asked Kellan.

"Eventually," said Josh.

"Meaning that she did not respond to them at first, but did so over time?" asked Patrick.

"Yes."

"How long did you send Miss Gatlin messages from the account of Craig Hutchins?"

Josh paused and thought. "A month? Maybe six weeks, I think."

"And did she agree to meet this imaginary Craig Hutchins for a date?" Kellan asked.

"Yes, finally," said Josh.

"Did anyone else know about this date?" asked Kellan.

"Sure." Josh smiled. "The whole gang was in on it."

"How did it happen?" asked Kellan.

"Macie coached me through setting it up," Josh said. "I'd show her the messages where Leslie wasn't so thrilled with the idea of meeting up, and she'd tell me exactly how to respond. She sort of made it my mission to get Leslie to agree to meet me for a date."

"Did she?" asked Kellan.

"Yes," said Josh. "She agreed to meet me at a park about halfway between Westport High and the high school Craig Hutchins supposedly went to."

"Did you meet Miss Gatlin alone?" asked Kellan.

"No. Of course not," said Josh. "Macie invited everyone. People brought popcorn and beers and blankets. She wanted everybody there to witness this one. Leslie showed up just after dark, at the time we'd agreed upon. The park Macie had picked was a private neighborhood park near her cousin's place. It's only open to the public during daylight hours, has a tall wrought-iron fence all the way around it. As soon as Leslie had waited for about thirty minutes, I walked up and introduced myself as Craig Hutchins, then I closed the gates on her and trapped her in the park with a bike lock."

"You locked her in the park?" asked Kellan.

"Yes," confirmed Josh. "Once I'd locked the gates, everybody who had come with us switched on their headlights and started whooping and throwing eggs at her, and Macie led everyone in a chant as well."

"What did Macie have you chant?" asked Kellan.

"'Kill yourself,'" said Josh. "It had sort of become her mantra with Leslie. She'd cough it in the hallway every time Leslie passed her."

"When did you let Leslie out of the park?" asked Kellan.

"We didn't," said Josh. "After Macie had everyone scream at her, she told Leslie that the park attendant would arrive at six a.m. and to have a good time camping."

I glanced over at Beth and saw that there were tears rolling down her cheeks. I pushed pause on the computer.

"Did that really happen?" I asked.

Beth nodded.

"Were you there?" I asked. "Were you, Jillian?"

Neither of them could look at me. Neither of them spoke. The silence was deafening.

"She was too embarrassed to even call her parents," said Beth, wiping her nose. "She texted them and told them that she was spending the night at Kelly's."

"How'd she get home the next morning?" I asked.

"Jake," said Jillian softly. "Leslie tried to call him and text him, but I swiped his phone from him so he wouldn't get the messages until morning. When he got up for his run, he saw the voice mails and jumped in his car to get her."

"I can't believe Josh copped to this," said Beth.

"You will," I said. "That's next."

I pushed play again, and Kellan Dirkson sprang to life on the screen.

"Why did you do this? If it was truly Macie's idea, why were you involved?"

Josh smiled at Kellan. "Does the name Marty Merrick ring a bell?"

"For the record, Marty Merrick is Macie's younger brother," Kellan said to the court reporter. "How is Marty Merrick pertinent to this case, Mr. Phillips?"

"Well, he got his drugs somewhere," said Josh.

"Are you insinuating that Marty Merrick bought drugs from you?" asked Kellan.

"Yes," said Josh.

"And Macie Merrick used this information to blackmail you?"

"One of Marty's friends let it slip to Macie that I was his supplier. She threatened to turn me in if I didn't set up the date with Leslie. I was about to place at state in the two hundred butterfly as a sophomore. I didn't want to get suspended. So I did what she said."

"Why come forward now? Is this about your romantic connection to the district attorney's daughter?"

"Objection!" Patrick's voice sounded frayed at the edges, like the threadbare afghan Aunt Liza used to cover her legs at church in the winter. "That's irrelevant, Kellan, and you know it."

"I don't think it's irrelevant," said Josh. "Macie Merrick played her ace yesterday. She got word to the DA that I was the one who supplied her brother's drugs. Mr. Braddock offered me two choices: charges on possession and trafficking, or coming clean in my deposition."

"So you're here to avoid jail time and probation?"

"Yes," said Josh. "I think the Merricks should know that if they don't settle this thing and it goes to trial, I have video of their son paying me for drugs that I'm sure they'd like to keep off the Internet right around the launch of the senator's race for US Congress."

"Again for the record," said Kellan, "you can produce this video?"

"I can produce it right now," said Josh. "What's your number, counsel? I can text you a link to it right now from my phone."

"No further questions," said Kellan.

The video ended. The three of us sat there staring at the black screen.

"Holy. Shit," said Beth. "Has Macie seen this?"

"No," I said. "I thought you two should see it first. Jillian, do you think I should show it to her?"

Jillian sat staring at the screen for a moment, then scrunched her eyes closed as if she were having a vision from a heavenly messenger.

"Let's see what Krista has to say."

23. BETH

Krista looked ridiculous in her deposition. For starters, she was missing her glasses, and her mother had forced her to go to a salon to get her hair colored and blown out for the interview. To top it all off, she was wearing a lavender twinset.

After the formalities, Kellan asked the question I'd been dreading since last night.

"Was Beth Patterson still friends with Leslie Gatlin when she helped you distract Leslie so that you could write on her locker?"

"Yes," said Krista.

"Why did she help you, then?" asked Kellan.

"Objection for the record," interjected Patrick. "Counsel is asking the witness to speculate."

"I'm just trying to find out about the nature of the relationship between the witness and Miss Patterson."

"Then just ask her that, for chrissakes, Kellan." Patrick rolled his eyes and took a swig of water. He was having a tough day, and it was about to get tougher.

"Are you currently friends with Beth Patterson?" Kellan asked, revising the question.

"Yes," said Krista.

"What is her role in your group, where Leslie is concerned?"

Krista jumped at the opportunity. "She was always sending messages to Leslie from a Facebook account she set up."

"Who participated in writing these messages?" asked Kellan.

Krista blinked at him like she didn't understand the question. "I'm sorry?"

"Did anyone besides Miss Patterson use this Facebook page to send messages to Miss Gatlin?"

"No," said Krista. "She was the 'send' girl. It was sort of her thing."

I reached over and paused the playback.

"Did she just say that?" I asked. "Did that really just happen?"

Jillian nodded. Katherine eyed me for a moment.

"What does Krista have against you, Beth?" Katherine was on to something.

I sighed. "She's about to tell you, I think." I pressed play.

"Did Miss Patterson host a party the week before Leslie Gatlin's death?" Kellan asked.

"Yes," said Krista. "It was her birthday."

"Did you attend the party?" Kellan asked.

"Yes."

"And you spent the night at Miss Patterson's after the party had ended?"

"Yes, I did," said Krista.

"Was Miss Gatlin also in attendance?" asked Kellan.

"I wouldn't say 'attendance,' exactly," said Krista. "But she showed up."

"Was she invited to the party?"

"No." Krista laughed.

"Why do you laugh when you say that?" asked Kellan.

"Because no one had hung out with her for over three years except Jake."

"So you were surprised to see her?"

"Uh . . . yes," scoffed Krista.

"Did anyone else see Leslie Gatlin at this party?"

"No. It was a small get-together. Just us girls. Beth's mom isn't into big parties."

"So just you and Beth saw her?"

"Yes. I'd gone to my car to get a sweatshirt I left in the backseat, when I saw Leslie walk up the front drive. Beth's house is on a corner, so I walked through the backyard to the hedge along Beth's driveway so I could see what was going on."

"And what happened?"

"Leslie was pleading with Beth about something. She was

trying to get her to take an envelope she was holding out."

"Did Miss Patterson take the envelope?" asked Kellan.

"No," said Krista. "She told Leslie that she shouldn't have come, and she begged her to leave, then she went back in the front door."

"What happened next?" asked Kellan.

"Leslie dropped to her knees on the front porch and cried for a minute. Then she put the envelope in the mailbox at the front door and left."

"Did you retrieve the envelope?"

"Yes," said Krista.

"Did you open it?"

"Yes."

"What was inside the envelope?"

"A letter," said Krista. "And a necklace."

"Will you please describe the necklace to me?"

"It was a silver chain with a tiny anchor on it."

"Did you give the letter and the necklace to Miss Patterson?"

"No," said Krista.

"Where are the letter and necklace now?"

"Macie took the necklace."

"You're referring to Macie Merrick, correct?" asked Kellan.

"Yes."

"What did she do with it?"

"She left the necklace on Jake's pillow with a note the night Leslie killed herself," said Krista.

"And the letter?" asked Kellan.

"We planned to give the letter to Beth, but then Leslie died the next week, and Macie told me to keep it quiet. She had a plan."

"Where is the letter now?" asked Kellan.

Krista pulled a lavender envelope out of her purse on the floor. "It's right here." She smiled.

"Would you please read what it says for us?"

I didn't wait for Krista to read the message. I didn't wait for the deposition to end, or for the video to stop, or the screen to get dark. I leaped from the bed, over Jillian and Katherine. I ran into the bathroom and slammed the door.

It's an odd thing, standing over the sink, staring into the mirror, knowing that your whole life has just changed. Your deepest secret is out.

How do I go back out there? How do I face Jillian? How does that conversation start?

I stood there staring at my own eyes in the mirror, trying to figure out what I would say.

Maybe: "I've been in love with Leslie since we were freshmen"?

Or how about: "Leslie didn't want me, so I hated her. Sure didn't think that was going to come up this morning when I left the house"?

I stared at myself for so long, I didn't recognize my own

face. My brain was numb. I was so tired. I'd been so scared for so long that this would happen—that somehow all of this would bubble up to the surface.

And now it had.

I realized how anxious I had been, because now the adrenaline—all the nervous energy that I'd put into hiding this for the past three years—was draining out of me. It felt so strange—so different than I had expected. It dawned on me that I didn't know what I had expected exactly. The visions of this thing with me and Leslie coming to light always ended in a fuzzy, dark haze of doom. There were no specifics. I'd spent so much time thinking about how to hide it that I hadn't thought at all about what not hiding it would be like. Now that it had actually happened, I began to wonder if it could possibly be any worse than the torture of hiding it—and all the things that had led to.

There was a timid knock on the door of the bathroom. I knew it was Jillian. I stayed at the sink and tried to think of how Leslie would handle this. She was so sure of herself in every way, it had seemed when I met her. I thought about the way I had kissed her in the garage that day Jake invited us to the pool party. Suddenly, the very idea of Leslie felt a thousand light-years away, and that made me feel sadder than I had the morning she died. I sat down on the edge of the bathtub and cried.

The second knock was firm and louder. I knew it was Katherine. I took a deep breath and swiped at my face. A glance back to the mirror proved that that was a hopeless gesture. I gripped the edge of the tub, squeezed my eyes shut, and said, “Come in.”

Jillian stuck her head in the door. “Is everything . . . okay?”

“No, Jills, everything is *not* okay. In fact, I don’t think I’ve ever felt like things were more screwed up in my life.”

“Well, while we’re sharing secrets, I’ve got one,” Katherine said, and turned to Jillian. “I sent Macie those pictures of you and Brad.”

“*What?*” Jillian and I shouted at the same time.

“*You* took those pictures?” Jillian’s jaw was hanging open.

“What pictures of you and Brad?” One look at Jillian’s face told me the whole story. “You mean you and Brad have been . . . ?” I couldn’t even finish the sentence.

“For three years now,” Katherine said. “Brad broke down and told Macie the whole story.”

“You’ve totally ruined my life!” Jillian almost shouted.

“No,” I said softly. “Jillian—she’s saved us.”

“What do you mean?” she asked. She had the look of a woman haunted.

“She did you a huge favor,” I said. “Now Macie doesn’t have anything over you.”

“Nobody needed to know about me and Brad,” said Jillian. I could see the heartbreak in her eyes.

Katherine looked at me, then over at Jillian.

"I wonder what did it?" she asked us. "What pushed Leslie over the edge?"

Jillian dropped her eyes to the computer and shrugged. "I don't know," she said, shaking her head. "The last Facebook message we sent from the Di Young account?"

"Yeah, but we sent one of those every week," said Katherine. "Who knows if she was even getting them?"

"Macie was always sending her text messages, too," I said.

"It could've been anything," Jillian said. "I guess we may never know."

24. JAKE

When I went back to Scarecrow Video to return the DVDs Brad and I had rented, Andy was standing at the counter. He was tall and skinny and had an encyclopedic knowledge of every horror movie ever made. Scarecrow Video had been a Capitol Hill institution since before I was born, and Andy was only about twenty-four, but when I think of the owners naming the store, I can't help but think they must've named it with him in mind. He was always wearing a baggy plaid flannel shirt and ripped jeans. It sort of looked like his clothes were wearing him. He was totally cool because he wasn't interested in being cool at all.

"Hey, brother," he said.

"Dude," I said. "*Evil Dead II* rocked my world."

He smiled, but there was something sad behind his eyes. "You doin' okay, man?" he asked.

There was no one else in the store at the moment. It was pretty quiet. I knew what he was talking about.

"Just didn't see you for a long time," he said. "Next thing I know, I'm talking to a bunch of lawyers."

I blinked at him, trying to understand. "Wait," I said. "You got a subpoena?"

"Yeah. I had a deposition earlier this week. What about you?"

"Mine's soon." We stood there quietly for a moment.

"What happened, man?" I looked up, startled somehow by his question. He put up both hands and stepped back. "Sorry—if you don't want to talk about it, you don't have to."

"No—it's . . . fine."

I took off my baseball cap and ran a hand through my hair, then put it back on.

"Andy?"

"Yeah, man?"

"What did they ask you about?"

He shrugged. "I dunno. Just if Leslie had friends. If I ever talked to her about what was going on with her, with school. If I'd noticed anything different or out of the ordinary. They kept calling her 'Miss Gatlin.' It was weird."

"What did you tell them?"

He looked at me for a second, then bit his lip and looked out the window. "Just . . . what I saw."

I waited. He kept looking at the window or down at his hands—anywhere but in my direction.

"I told 'em that I didn't think she was having a great time at school, but that she didn't really talk about it much. Not with me, at least. I knew that she liked a couple of the girls on her volleyball team. The only thing that changed really was you." He looked me straight in the eyes, then back at the parking lot. "Where'd you go, man?"

"What do you mean?" I asked.

"Well, I just know that she really liked you. Liked hanging with you. Was always talking about playing the guitar with you. Right after Christmas you guys had that talk in the car. I remember it was raining. She ran out and got in your ride on her break. It was dark, but you had the dome light on and I could see you guys talking. You seemed upset when she came running back in. You followed her up to the door, and when she came in, you just stood there, watching her through the window. You were totally drenched, but you didn't seem to notice."

I looked down at my sneakers. At that moment, I wanted to be running through the neighborhood, away from my house, face full up to the sun and the blinding white light of the rays as they bounced off the snow that still blanketed the upper half of Mount Hood. I needed to feel the rhythm in my legs, the swell in my lungs, the burn in my chest.

Andy looked back at me. "What happened?"

My legs tensed as if they might carry me into a spring out the front door of Scarecrow Video and far away from . . . what? Andy? This conversation?

The voice in my head cut through the pounding in my ears with the answer:

The truth.

When I pulled up to Scarecrow, the rain was coming down so hard, my windshield wipers weren't keeping up.

I texted Leslie: `Here.`

I could barely make out her figure in the window. The store was deserted. An old-fashioned movie rental place was no match for streaming Netflix when a Seattle thunderstorm was involved.

As I saw her approach the front door and pull up her hood, I smiled. Even in a raincoat she looked like dynamite. It had been so much fun watching her play volleyball this season. Brad kept giving me crap when I dragged him to her matches on Saturday mornings after we'd been up late partying after a Friday-night football game.

She was easily the best player on the team. The fact that she was easy on the eyes was just icing on the cake.

Suddenly she burst through the passenger-side door, all raindrops and umbrella, drenching my shirt as she leaned over the console for a hug.

"Oh my God. I'm so wet," she said. "Can you believe this?" She gazed up through the windshield.

"No, I can't," I said, staring at the way her blond hair brushed her neck as she craned it upward to see the sheets of water pouring off the roof of the building.

She turned to look at me, and I met her lips with mine. She jumped a bit and pulled away. "Okay, wasn't expecting that."

I smiled at her. "There's probably a lot you don't expect about me. Or suspect."

"Stop it, Jake."

"What?" I smiled at her, but I was confused.

She ran a hand through her damp hair. "I have wet socks now because you just had to talk to me in the middle of my shift," she said. "What's so important?"

I glanced down at my thumbs mindlessly tapping out a beat on the steering wheel. "I know I haven't been around a lot lately," I began.

"Jake, I—"

"Look, don't say anything right now," I said, cutting her off. "Just hear me out on this."

She looked down at her hands in her lap and let out a deep breath.

"Okay. I've got fifteen minutes."

"Look, I know I haven't been around as much, but I've come to every volleyball game, and all week I look forward to that and playing guitar with you. All I think about is you. We're more than friends, Les, and you know it."

She looked out into the rain. "We are more than just friends, Jake, but—"

"No 'buts'!" I smacked the steering wheel.

"Jake—what do you want from me?"

I blinked and looked her straight in the eyes. "I don't want anything 'from' you, Leslie. I want you. Just you. I want you to be my girlfriend."

She held my gaze and my right hand. There was something missing in her eyes, something that had been there once. She reached up and touched my face. Her hand was cool on my cheek and I realized how warm I was.

As her hand slipped off my cheek, she pulled out her phone.

"I want to show you something," she said.

She tapped into her text messages and pulled up a number with an area code I didn't recognize, and turned the screen to me so that I could read the texts:

Slut

Boy stealer

Bitch face

Man eater

Why are ur thighs so fat?

Nice rack. Still screwing the doc?

My cheeks burned. "What the hell is that?" I asked. "Whose number is that?"

"I don't know for sure," she said softly, slipping the phone back into the pocket of her jacket.

"Leslie, let me see that."

"It doesn't matter, Jake. Whoever is doing this uses a different Google Voice number every time. I've tried to report it. I've told my mom about it. I've told the wireless company. We've emailed Google. The person just changes to a new one and the texts keep coming."

"It's Macie, isn't it?"

Leslie stared out the window. "Probably," she said quietly. "But there's no way to prove it."

"How long has this been going on?" Rage boiled up inside me like an explosion.

"For a while," sighed Leslie.

"Macie is always at our house with Jillian, and vice versa. How do I not know about this?"

Leslie glanced my way and laughed a little, shaking her head.

"What?" I asked.

"You're so sweet, Jake. You just move through the world assuming the best about people. Nobody tells you otherwise."

"Who else knows about this?"

"You think they'd admit it to me? I'm sure the whole gang knows. I'm sure they keep it from you. I'm sure it isn't hard."

"That's it!" I yelled, and pounded the steering wheel. Leslie jumped. I was already dialing my phone.

"What are you doing?" she asked.

"Calling Jillian. This has to stop."

"*No!* Jake, don't." She grabbed my phone and tapped end call.

"Dammit, Leslie, give me my phone!"

"Jake, look at me," she said. Then, when my eyes locked on hers, she said quietly, "You can't bring this up. You cannot tell anyone, do you understand?"

"You're crazy if you think I'm going to sit around while that bitch harasses you, and my sister and best friend follow her around like a puppy dog."

"If you bring it up, it will just get worse." She was desperate. Her eyes searched mine wildly for some sign that I wouldn't talk about it.

"How can it get any worse?" I asked. "After that stunt in the park, Josh Phillips still crosses to the other side of the hall when he sees me."

"And remember what happened?" Leslie asked, the fire back in her eyes. "You got called in and threatened with a suspension."

"Josh is such an asshole." I shook my head.

We sat quietly for a minute listening to the rain pound the roof of the car. The windows were fogged up because of our voices, my yelling, her sentences, soft but firm. Our breath had mixed—little particles of the moisture from deep inside our bodies had been showered out into this tiny space and mingled with one another, then clung to the cool glass in tiny beads. There we were; Leslie and I mixed up together on the windows, fogging our view of anything else but each other.

I wanted her so badly in that moment. I wanted us to be mixed up, our arms, our legs, our lips—not just our breath.

I reached over and smoothed her bangs away from her forehead. She closed her eyes and rested her cheek against my hand.

As I leaned in to kiss her, she opened her eyes and put a hand on my chest to stop me.

"If you go to Jillian or to Macie, this just gets worse."

"And if you won't be my girlfriend, *this* gets worse," I said, thumping my fist against my chest. "This tightness in my lungs. This ache in my gut. Leslie, I can't breathe."

"Macie would flip her shit if you started going out with me. Jake, haven't you been paying attention? This is what started the whole thing. You didn't want to date her. This whole thing comes down to what Macie wants. She wants you."

"I don't care what Macie wants." My voice was so low and so intense when it came out of me that I almost didn't recognize myself.

"She does," said Leslie quietly. "If she can't have you, no one else can either."

I was quiet for a long time. I felt the fight drain out of me, and with it, the hopelessness of the situation flooded into its place. Suddenly I was desperate. Desperate to keep her here with me, in the car, in this moment.

But all I could say was, "Please."

"What?" she asked.

"Please don't let Macie win."

She shoved her hands into her raincoat pockets. "Break's over," she whispered.

Before I knew what was happening, she was running toward the front door of the video store, and somehow I was chasing her—no umbrella, no jacket. The rain was cold, like nails being driven into my cheeks and neck and shoulders. She got to the door ahead of me and slipped inside and behind the counter as a group of hipster college kids pushed out into the rain. I was blocked from entering by a barrage of fedoras and umbrellas. As the doors closed behind them, I looked up to see Leslie disappear into the romance section.

Is she crying? Or is there just rain still on her cheeks?

I couldn't tell for sure through the glass of the doors. Andy turned around at the counter and saw me. Suddenly I realized I was crying. He raised his hand and started toward me. I watched him coming over like it was a cold, wet nightmare. He pushed open the door and yelled over the storm, "Hey, man! You okay?"

I shook my head in a silent no. *No. No, I am not okay. Nothing is okay.*

Then I slowly turned and walked into the parking lot, raising my arms and face up to the cold rain, letting the chill tear through me, wishing it would somehow put out the fire.

"So you pretty much stopped coming around at that point, I guess," said Andy. "Makes sense now. I wouldn't want to hang with the chick who broke my heart, either."

"That's what made it worse," I said. "I wanted to be with her every minute. I just wanted her near me. I'd still go watch her volleyball games. Beth would show up and sit next to me on the bleachers. We didn't even talk—really, we hardly spoke—just sat and watched Leslie. We'd both leave early."

I paused to swallow the lump that had come up in my throat. "I wish we'd stuck around," I said. "I'm not sure she ever knew we were there."

"Did you see her before . . . ?" Andy's question trailed off into the awful nothing that happens when the sentence becomes too terrible to continue to say out loud.

I nodded. "I was the last person who talked to her that I know of," I said.

"Heavy," Andy whispered. "Did she call you?"

I shook my head. The words were getting harder to find. Why was I telling Andy this? What was it? I realized that he was the only person I knew who knew Leslie but didn't know the rest of the people involved in the story. Something about him was real, genuine. He'd gone to a deposition about Leslie's death, not as the accused, but as a friend, a coworker, somebody willing to help out.

"I just showed up and knocked on her door," I said.

"Just like that, huh? Right outta the blue?"

"No," I said quietly.

"What made you go?" Andy asked.

"The necklace," I said. "We bought these necklaces." I pulled mine out of my shirt. "Me and Leslie and Jillian—when we were in Cape Cod the summer before ninth grade."

Andy frowned. "I don't understand," he said. "You had Leslie's necklace?"

"No," I said. "Macie did."

I'll never forget walking up the stairs that night. I'd been at Brad's playing video games. I'd seen all the cars out front, and I knew that Jillian had the girls over. I didn't feel like talking to them, so I was as quiet as possible.

I walked into the bathroom between our rooms, and as I was turning the lock in the door that led to Jillian's room, I realized that something had been strange when I'd passed through my bedroom. There was something on my pillow.

I stepped back out of the bathroom and walked over to the head of my bed. There was a pink three-by-five card that read, *If I can't have what I want, you can't have what you want.*

I frowned and reached down to pick up the card. Underneath it was a wad of silver chain. As I lifted it from the pillow, a tiny silver anchor fell against my palm.

I don't remember ever seeing a color before. I've heard the expression "I saw red," meaning "I was angry," but there was more to this color—it was darker than red. It was crimson—so dark it was almost purple. It was six quick steps down the hall to Jillian's bedroom.

When I threw open the door, it hit the wall so hard that the lamp fell off Jillian's dresser, and Krista shrieked. Beth was sitting at the computer, and when Katherine asked what I was holding, I wanted to yell at the top of my lungs. I wanted to put my fist through the wall.

Before I could move, I heard Macie say that I was "so sexy" when I'm angry, and something about the glint in her eye confirmed what I already knew: M AAAacie put this necklace here.

I had so many questions, they were tripping over one another in my brain.

"Don't ever speak to me again," I said. "I want you out of my life."

Then I raced down the stairs to my car and squealed away from the curb toward Leslie's.

25. JILLIAN

"What are we doing here?" Beth's face was ashen as she stared out of the car at the Highline Performing Arts Center.

"We are here to support Katherine," I said.

We both sat there looking blankly at the building for another minute in complete silence, watching parents and grandparents and friends and relatives and sisters, and older brothers who were excited for the swimsuit competition, and little brothers who were dragged there, as they filed from the parking lot into the building for the Miss Washington Teen USA Pageant.

"Do we have to go in there?" Beth asked. "Katherine will be onstage. She'll have lights in her eyes. She'll never know if we were here or not."

"Macie will," I said.

"I don't care," said Beth. "I don't ever want to see her again."

"Unfortunately, you will. Besides, we promised," I said. "This is it. If Katherine wins Miss Washington Teen, she goes to Miss Teen USA. Besides, if we don't show up after the last twenty-four hours, Macie wins."

Beth sighed. "This used to be so fun. I love watching Katherine in these pageants. She's so poised and pretty, and personable."

"Nice alliteration." I smiled.

"Perfect."

I laughed. "C'mon. Let's get in there."

Macie and Krista were coming out of the bathroom when we walked into the lobby, and when we saw them, Beth and I stopped in our tracks. I could feel my stomach sweep up into the back of my throat and then free-fall into my toes in the one one-hundredth of a second that it took for my brain to get the signals from my eyes that it was Macie standing there with Krista at her side, staring in my direction—directly into my eyes.

Everything went silent behind a roar in my ears. It was like I was seeing Macie again for the first time, and I remembered kindergarten—Miss Keeler's class. The Merricks had just moved to the school district so that Mr. Merrick could run for the city council seat there, but I didn't know that yet. I was outside at recess on the first day of school, in the four-square lines with a kickball, getting ready to serve, when I saw her walk out onto the playground.

Macie stopped and looked across the blacktop, and when we locked eyes, we just stared at each other for a second. Then I smiled. I'm still not sure why. She smiled back and raised her hand, waved like she'd known me for years, and ran toward me. That afternoon, we waited for our moms on the curb together in the pick-up line, and she gave me a sticker and called Jake a "fart monster," and that made me laugh so hard I cried. The rest just sort of happened.

We'd survived chicken pox in fifth grade together, and Robby Garret telling everybody he made out with us at his birthday party in sixth grade. We'd even made it through last year, when she decided to run for student council president with Katherine instead of me.

Now, here we were, seeing each other again—for the first time. She knew about Brad, and about Beth, and as we locked eyes, everything went silent and I felt this place inside me open up. Like an hourglass there were little particles rushing out of me—was it strength or courage or hope? All I knew was that I was desperate to stop it from draining away from me.

And in that moment—as we held each other's gaze across the lobby—I felt my heart racing and my stomach dropping. I suddenly wondered how I'd gotten here to this place where the fear of losing my history made me risk my future. And in spite of it all, I took a deep breath.

Then I smiled.

I'm still not sure why.

She smiled back and raised her hand, waved like she'd known me for years, and ran toward me.

The rest just sort of happened.

Katherine was gorgeous and flawless until the interview portion of the evening gown competition—usually her strongest category.

Surrounded by girls in spangles and Mylar and bugle beads, Katherine entered the stage at the top of the staircase in a simple red organza sheath, the color of blood. Both the neck and back draped in a low swag, her mocha skin glowed, solitaire earrings sparkled in the spotlight, and a single strand of diamonds glittered at her neck. The dress clung to her lightly, all the way down to diamond-studded Jimmy Choo high-heel sandals that flashed with each step as they peeked out from beneath her hem. A slight flared train flirted with the floor behind her as she walked.

Katherine's hair was twisted up like Audrey Hepburn's, and her long, red fingernails barely brushed her thighs as she easily walked down the stairs; the air under her arms perfectly highlighted her figure. She didn't walk. She floated.

All the other contestants in the top ten had been greeted with cheers and whistles and little brothers with air horns when they were announced for the evening gown/interview portion of the pageant. Before anyone cheered for Katherine, there was a gasp and a silence, and then a roar that rivaled the moment Beth nailed the dismount for her beam routine at the meet last year.

When she reached the microphone, she smiled and nodded to the judges. The emcee, Vince Grayson, the weatherman for the FOX News affiliate in Seattle, had to wait for the cheering to stop before he asked her the question. Macie's eyes were glued to the stage, her jaw turned up. Our seats were in the fourth row, on the right side of the center section. I looked over at her when she reached out to grab my hand. She kept staring right at Katherine, and then Vince was reading Katherine's question—the question that had been chosen for her at random.

"Katherine, the issue of cyber-bullying has been in the news lately with a rash of recent teen suicides across the country, one reported here in Seattle. Have you or any of your friends ever been the target of cyber-bullying, and if so, what would you do as Miss Washington Teen to reach out to those both perpetrating and suffering from online bullying?"

I couldn't breathe. I felt a sharp pain in my left hand and realized that Macie was squeezing it so tightly I thought she was going to break my fingers, but I couldn't move. The entire auditorium sat in silence as the question echoed across the stage and landed in our collective ears like an atom bomb. No one made a sound. No one moved.

Katherine's smile slowly faded. Her shoulders, which had

been thrust back in a perfect pageant stance at the microphone, drifted downward as she seemed to study the diamond strap across the toes of her right foot.

As the pause grew longer and more uncomfortable, Vince hesitantly raised his microphone again. "Katherine?" he asked from the podium at the side of the stage.

When she looked up, the lights hit the tears that were running down Katherine's cheeks.

She looked out at the audience, up to the balcony, and then directly toward the four of us sitting in the fourth row. Then she looked down at the judges and leaned into the microphone.

There was no well-trained smile. There was no practiced prose. There was just a gorgeous girl, in a red dress, crying.

"There was a girl at my school," Katherine said softly. "Her name was Leslie. She was beautiful, and she killed herself." Katherine's voice cracked, and she looked down at her feet again. She took a deep breath and tapped beneath her eyes to try to wipe the tears without smearing her eyeliner.

She brought her head up with the same resolve that I had seen that day when she told Macie that Leslie's parents were suing us. "She was bullied," said Katherine, her shoulders back again. "She was bullied by people I knew, by my best friends. And instead of stopping them, I joined them."

She looked down at the judges. "I was afraid. I was afraid that my best friends wouldn't like me anymore. I wasn't strong enough to say no."

Beth was crying quietly on my right. Macie's vise grip on my hand had turned tighter. Krista was staring at the stage with her jaw unhinged.

Katherine turned to address the panel of judges. "I don't deserve to represent the state of Washington at a pageant or anywhere else. I'm removing myself from the competition tonight. I wanted to apologize publicly and say that this will be my final pageant."

A hush fell over the auditorium. Katherine stared up into the lights above the balcony.

"Leslie Gatlin, wherever you are . . . I'm sorry."

Then she gazed out at the audience one final time, turned, and stepped out of the spotlight.

The audience was stunned. Macie immediately let go of my hand and began texting. Krista put her face into her hands. Beth dropped her tissue and was reaching under her chair for it. I realized I was the only one watching as Katherine stepped away from the microphone and did her required walk and turn before heading back up the stairs and through the set to the offstage area.

She walked with a stride I had never witnessed: a slow, steady boldness filled with resolve. It was as if she weren't alone on that stage. It was like she was leading an army of people behind her. In that moment I would've followed her anywhere.

She had never been more beautiful.

• • •

Brad was sitting next to Macie and Krista in the booth at Marv's when Beth and I arrived.

"Hi." I smiled. He nodded and looked away.

Macie slapped her phone down onto the table.

"When is Katherine getting here?"

"Is she coming?" asked Beth weakly.

"If she knows what's good for her," said Macie. "God, after that stunt tonight, I could just brain her."

"Stunt?" I asked with a frown.

"Oh, please!" Macie shook her head and rolled her eyes at the ceiling. "Don't tell me you bought that load of crap!"

"I don't think it was crap," said Beth.

"Oh, gimme a break," said Krista.

"I don't think she was acting," I said quietly.

Macie opened her mouth to say something, then I saw her eyes turn to behind me. "Well, here she comes," she said quietly.

I turned around and ran toward Katherine. I threw both arms around her in the middle of the restaurant.

"Hi," she whispered.

"You were amazing," I said.

She smiled at me shyly, then we turned around and walked to the table.

Macie crossed her arms in the booth. "You know, you'd probably be Miss Washington Teen right now if you hadn't pulled that stunt during your interview," she said.

Katherine looked at her and shook her head. "When are you gonna get it, Macie?"

Macie's chin dropped and her eyebrows shot up. "When am I gonna get what?"

"That this is over," said Katherine.

"Oh, nothing is over, VP," said Macie. "Your deposition is on Monday afternoon, is it not? And mine is on Tuesday. When we're done, the Gatlins won't have a case, and this will all go away. In the end, we'll go back to school, and things will quiet down. We'll be back to normal before you know it," she sneered at Katherine.

Katherine squinted at Macie and said, "Normal? Macie, there is no more 'normal.' Our reputations are falling apart."

"Well, yours is, at least," said Macie. "You made sure of that tonight in front of fifteen hundred people and the local media."

"Macie, you know that reporter who broke the story on Marty's stint in rehab in the *Seattle Times*? Steve Garrison?"

"What about him?" asked Macie.

"Josh Phillips got a call from Mr. Garrison, and Josh is talking. They're planning a huge cover story about high school bullying and how Braddock is going to crack down. He's talking big about criminal charges in bullying cases."

"He wouldn't dare," said Macie smugly.

"I don't know what you think you have on Graham Braddock, but his daughter Elaine is pushing him to come down hard on this issue. Apparently high school was no picnic for her."

"Well, the DA can decide to do what he wants, but if he pushes this, my dad is ready with a few financial statements from Mr. Braddock's last campaign," said Macie fiercely.

"And Josh Phillips is ready with a video of your brother," said Katherine quietly.

For the first time all night, Brad actually looked at me. "What?" he asked.

"Ask Macie," Katherine said. "She tipped off Braddock. She told him that Josh was Marty's pot supplier. She's been holding this over him since ninth grade, and she tried to hit him where it hurt."

Katherine paused and slid into the booth. She looked at Macie, whose eyes were narrowed and her jaw clenched.

"Only, Macie's plan backfired. The DA gave Josh immunity for testifying about the video during his deposition," Katherine explained.

"What video?" Macie asked.

"Josh has video of Marty exchanging cash for drugs. When your dad's people called Braddock to tell him that his daughter's boyfriend was a drug dealer, he sat Josh down and gave him a hard choice. If Josh talks to this reporter, your dad will never run for anything again."

"There is no video," scoffed Macie. "Besides. How do you know any of this?"

"I've seen his deposition."

Macie leaped to her feet and toward Katherine. The table jumped, knocking water glasses everywhere. Suddenly we were all on our feet, and Macie was shouting.

"You've seen his deposition? You are a liar! You told me that you couldn't get the video. My dad's lawyers want to see that footage. You're going to ruin our lives!"

It seemed like it was taking every bit of strength Brad had to hold Macie back against the bench. Macie smacked at his chest. "Let me go!"

"Stop it, Macie," he said.

In the silence, Katherine shouldered her purse. "Macie, Leslie's life was the one that got ruined. Have you ever considered that maybe this actually is our fault? I didn't d serve to be on that stage. I wasn't beautiful to Leslie. Mayb all deserve what we're getting. Look at the pain we've cau ."

Krista slumped into the booth on the other side of Macie. Katherine turned to me. "Thanks for coming tonight." She smiled.

As she turned to leave, I heard Macie growl from the booth, "Where do you think you're going, bitch?"

Katherine stopped but didn't turn around. "What did you call me, Macie?"

"Monday morning, you're over," spat Macie.

Katherine turned around slowly and looked at each of us in turn before walking back to the table. "Macie, this has been over since the morning Leslie killed herself."

Then she walked away.

Macie started laughing, first quietly, then she giggled hysterically like a crazy person.

"Oh my *God*!" she exclaimed, wiping tears from her eyes. "You know what I think?" she said with a big, bright smile. "I think that Katherine obviously feels guilty. Maybe it's time to come clean in our depositions, eh, Jillian?"

"What do you mean?" I asked.

"I think it's time to tell the lawyers the truth, the whole truth, and nothing but the truth: Katherine was the mastermind behind all of this."

Beth stood up quietly and slipped into her hoodie, then picked up her purse. "Macie, did you see what happened onstage tonight? That was Katherine being more honest than any of us have ever had the nerve to be. It's on video. All of it. And I bet by the time we get home, it's on the news."

"What is that supposed to mean?" Macie asked.

I looked at her as I pulled out my keys. I searched her face for some sign of the girl from the playground. I couldn't find her. Even her eyes were different.

"It means you're on your own here, Macie," I said quietly.

Then I followed Beth toward the door that led to the parking lot, and took the first step away from my past and into my future.

26. KATHERINE

Aunt Liza sent me a text message as I was parking for my deposition at Daddy's firm on Monday. It made me laugh because she's the last woman in the world I expected would start texting.

In all caps, the message read: REMEMBER WHAT AUDREY SAID.

I smiled to myself and took a deep breath. I had been honest in front of the whole world. If I could do that, I could drop my poker face in front of the lawyers here today.

Out of habit, I pulled the rearview mirror over to check my makeup, then smiled at myself when I heard what I knew Aunt Liza would say.

You didn't lose your pretty since last time you checked, sugar.

I fixed the mirror, grabbed my purse, and opened the car door.

• • •

Daddy walked me to the door of the conference room, then turned to me in the hall and dropped his chin until we were nose to nose. His eyes were warm and clear.

"You know I love you, no matter what." His voice was a husky whisper, like a warm sweater on a cold night. I wrapped my arms around him, and he rested his chin on my head. "Nothing you could ever do would change that."

"How can you be sure?" The voice that left my mouth was thin and reedy. I wasn't a beauty queen under lights with perfect poise. I was a little girl shaking on the inside, hoping this big bear of a man would be able to prop me up.

"My sister Liza was right, sweetheart. You're more than just brains and beauty. You have special ears that always hear what's right."

As he walked away, he turned and gave me a thumbs-up. "I'll be in my office when you're done."

I stood there in the hall for a moment, listening to the ring of his shoes on the tile as he strode down to his office. Behind the door in front of me was the true test. All I had to do was listen for the truth, then say it out loud.

Time to drop my poker face and show my cards.

I walked into the room and shook hands all around the table.

I raised my hand and swore to Lauren Wolinsky and God that I would tell the whole truth.

Then I sat down, and Kellan Dirkson started in with the questions.

I told him the whole story. How I met Macie and how Macie pulled a fast one on Jillian and made me her running mate for student government. How she convinced me that all I needed to get into the pageant scene was the help of one woman, Denise Gatlin, and how her daughter was in desperate need of a friend.

I told Kellan Dirkson that Macie had grinned at me when she said this, like a possum eatin' briars, and at that moment, that voice I hear when I listen on my insides was hollering that this Macie Merrick was trouble, but I didn't listen. I wanted to be Miss Washington Teen, and I was going to meet this Leslie girl and become her friend if it killed me.

"But it didn't kill me," I said softly. "It killed Leslie."

As I said this, something broke inside me, and I guess Patrick saw I was about to tip my hand, 'cause he jumped up and objected and sputtered and choked and tried to have all sorts of things stricken from the record. Kellan matched him yell for yell, and in all the fuss, I looked up and caught the eye of Lauren Wolinsky, who was sitting real still across that big, white lacquered conference table. As the men hollered like someone had set fire to their suit pants, she fixed me with the softest, gentlest, kindest smile—a real smile, not a pageant grin for the cameras, but a beautiful, genuine smile. It was an Aunt Liza smile, a smile that silently whispered, *I can hear you, and you're telling the truth.*

Then Lauren Wolinsky stood up, smacked a legal pad against that big, shiny table with the force of an Old Testament prophet, and bellowed the words "*Cool it*" like she was a linebacker possessed by Satan himself. Both of those men stopped dead in their tracks and looked at her, slack-jawed and wide-eyed.

Once it was quiet, Ms. Wolinsky took her seat, flipped a golden curtain of hair over her shoulder, and crossed her legs. "Gentlemen, I think we should listen to what Katherine has to say. A girl committed suicide, and Katherine has been kind enough to come here and tell us the truth."

Patrick was quiet. Kellan was quiet. Both of them sat.

"Now, then, Katherine, please continue," said Lauren.

I nodded. I wiped my eyes, and then I looked at Lauren Wolinsky, and I explained how I had thought it would be hard to be friends with Leslie, but that it was easier than anything I had ever done. I'd sat next to her at the lab tables in chemistry and we became partners. The next step was studying at her house, and then letting it slide in the kitchen that I was the reigning Miss Atlanta Teen, and at that point, Denise Gatlin had tripped around the corner with her ever-present glass of pinot grigio and exclaimed, "Katherine! We have got a lot to talk about!"

And we did. Turns out Mrs. Gatlin was a board member for the Miss Washington Teen USA Pageant circuit. She knew every judge, coach, talent consultant, makeup artist, and hair stylist that mattered. She knew who would judge what when. She knew how to make sure her daughter's best friend met them before the regional competitions.

Turns out she knew every bartender at the events too, and the night I won Miss Seattle Teen my junior year, she was supposed to welcome the audience with a word about the pageant organization before she introduced the host. Instead, she was backstage in my dressing room with a bottle of Veuve and the hunky bartender I'd tipped to take it to her.

"So you purposefully set her up?" Kellan asked. "Why? What happened?"

"I ran to get the stage manager and told him what was going on in my dressing room," I said. "He got the chairman of the board. They both found her in there together."

Kellan was silent for a moment. "Due respect, Katherine, but . . . who cares?"

"I don't understand the question," I said.

"So a board member for a pageant gets tanked and makes out with a bartender in a contestant's dressing room. So what? Big deal. Who cares?"

I looked down at my hands, folded on the table in front of me. "Leslie," I said quietly. "Leslie cared."

"Yeah, but who would know about this?" Kellan was driving at something.

"Everyone," I said. "Macie was backstage with me that night. She snapped a picture of Mrs. Gatlin and the bartender in my dressing room when the board chairman opened the door. By the time I got to school the next morning, she'd posted it all over Facebook. She uploaded the picture of Mrs. Gatlin hunkered down on this boy, with the words, 'Now we know where Leslie learned to be a whore.'"

"What did Leslie do?" Kellan asked quietly.

"She actually tried to apologize to me," I said. "She came up to me in the hall the next morning and said, 'Congratulations, Katherine.' Before I could turn around from my locker, Macie was flappin' her mouth."

"What did Macie say?"

I swallowed hard and glanced up at Lauren Wolinsky. She was looking directly into my eyes, and when I met her gaze, she nodded at me, just once.

"I don't remember all of it," I said. "But I remember how it ended. She just looked at Leslie and said, 'Kill yourself.'"

"What happened?" asked Kellan.

"Leslie teared up," I said.

"And what did you say?"

"Nothing," I whispered.

"I thought you were friends with Leslie," said Kellan. "Why didn't you say anything?"

"I was afraid," I said. "Macie's voice was louder than the one inside me. The one I should have listened to instead."

The room was quiet for a moment. Patrick looked at Kellan. "Are we done here?" he asked.

"Yes," said Kellan. "I believe we are."

27. BETH

I suppose it was inevitable that I'd run into Jake at some point. I mean, we went to the same school and we were in the same class, and turned out Jillian was becoming the only friend I had left.

I guess I assumed it would be in class, or in the hallway outside the locker rooms, when I was getting ready for practice and he was leaving the weight room.

I never thought it would be at Leslie's grave. I mean, really—doesn't that seem a little on the nose?

But there we were, on a day so sunny, it defied description: the girl who wanted Leslie, and the boy who wanted Leslie—standing at the edge of the leveled patch of fresh soil, staring at the granite marker that had just been delivered that week:

Leslie Gatlin
1993–2011

I'd stopped at Trader Joe's for some flowers on the way over, and had just laid a bouquet of daffodils at the foot of the stone when I heard him walking up behind me. He was wearing a Seahawks hoodie and carrying a single rose with a long green stem that exploded in deep crimson velvet. He stopped next to me and stood there for a moment staring at the tombstone. Then he bent down and placed the rose next to my daffodils, stood up again, and put his hands into the hoodie pocket.

The sun seemed to mock us, standing at the tombstone under a cloudless sky. The rays were warm, but the wind off the sound was just brisk enough that it made me glad I had worn a jacket. I pulled it a little closer, not so much for warmth as for the secure feeling that I get from the layers of fabric wrapped tightly around me. It's a trick I learned when I was little at gymnastic meets in giant, drafty gymnasiums. I felt something even warmer across my shoulders, and I realized that it was Jake's arm.

We stood there in silence for what seemed like a very long time. I looked out toward Mount Hood in the distance, and the bright sun glaring off the snow brought tears to my eyes. Or maybe it was hearing Jake sniff, and glancing up at him from behind my dark glasses and realizing that there were silent tears running down his cheeks. Slowly I brought my arm up around his waist, then leaned my face against his chest and sobbed.

When the tears had subsided, I took off my sunglasses and wiped at my eyes with my sleeve. Jake's jaw was tight. He was angry. I'd seen this before, the night that Leslie died, when he'd burst into Jillian's bedroom like a rocket, holding that necklace.

"Jake?" I reached out to touch his arm.

He turned away, raising his face to the sky and yelling out a long, slow cry. It wasn't hurt. It was rage.

"I'm so angry," he panted at me through his tears, his face flushed, his eyes rimmed with red. "I'm so angry and I'm so sad, and I'm angry at myself for being sad, and I'm sad that I feel so angry."

I was quiet for a second. I looked back over my shoulder at the sound and the skyline and the ferry headed out to Bainbridge Island.

This is what it comes down to. You deserve this.

"Jake." My voice was a whisper. "I'm so sorry. I know you should be angry at me, I just—"

"You?" He almost laughed. "Angry at you? I'm angry at *her*. I'm so mad at her for pulling this shit."

He jammed his hands deeper into the hoodie as if he had to anchor himself to the ground and scrunched his eyes closed as if he could will himself into another moment in time, a moment already passed, a moment where he could do something, say something, to change what he was feeling here and now.

"You're angry at Leslie?" I asked.

"How could she be so selfish?" His shoulders were shaking and his eyes were still closed. "How could she think that this would solve anything?"

He sat down on the grass at the edge of the dirt square and hugged his knees to his chest. "If I'd just paid attention. I keep thinking I could have figured this out. I could have somehow understood. She just kept sending me away. She just kept saying, 'You don't understand,' but I could've understood if she'd given me a chance. I would've tried. I think of all the times I went running to get her off my mind. I should've run to her place. I should've gotten to the bottom of it. I'm so angry at myself, and I'm so angry at her for not telling me."

I sank down on a spot of grass across from him.

"Jake, this isn't your fault. If it's anybody's fault, it's mine."

Jake looked directly at me. "You're damn right it is," he said. It was so low, I wasn't sure that I had heard him. "It's your fault, and Macie's and Jillian's and Katherine's and Krista's." His voice cracked again. "And mine."

"Jake, I'm so sorry. I can't say enough that I'm sorry. I'll never be able to say it enough to bring her back. I was just so scared. I didn't know what to do."

"You should have loved her!" Jake shouted, and looked away from me. "You should've loved her. How could that have been so hard?"

"I did. I did, Jake."

He looked back at me with a sneer. "Coulda fooled me," he scoffed. "You could've been her friend. Instead you turned on her for not loving you the way you wanted."

Suddenly I was up on my feet, hands clenched, shouting, "You don't understand. I didn't know what to do. I didn't know how to be . . . like that. I couldn't risk her telling . . ." I stopped short and dropped my head.

"Macie?" Jake asked. "That's what you were going to say, wasn't it? Goddamn that Macie Merrick. What kind of fucking evil witchcraft does that girl hold over you and my sister? What did she ever do for you?"

"Yes!" I yelled back. "Fine. Yes, I didn't know how to go up to Macie and say, 'Stop picking on Leslie. I love her.' My God, Jake. Look what Macie did to Leslie. All I could think is what she'd do to me."

Jake hid his face with his hand and sat quietly for a minute. Then he sniffed and spit and wiped his eyes with the heel of his palm.

"I just knew that what was going on inside me was all wrong," I said.

Jake's face snapped toward mine and exploded. "There is nothing wrong with what's going on *inside* you," he shouted. "It was what you let go on *outside* you that mattered. Lying about it was wrong. Not being who you are was wrong. Caring more about what Macie Merrick thought than about what you felt was wrong."

"Shut up!" I was frantic. My voice was shrill and terrified. "Jake, you don't know what she can do. You don't know what Macie is capable of. I knew that there was no way I could stand up for Leslie and risk her telling anyone what had happened. Not now. Not here. It was just too . . ."

"Hard?" Jake's eyes narrowed when he said it.

He stood up and grabbed the bouquet of daffodils I'd brought and shook them at me. "Harder than this, Beth? Harder than *this*?"

He threw the flowers back at the base of the granite marker. They sprayed apart in a wild flash of green and gold.

"*Nothing* could be harder than *this*," he said. His voice was eerie and quiet. I looked up, and as he stared at the dates etched forever in the stone, the tension seemed to drain out of him, like someone had pulled the stopper on an air mattress. Right before my eyes, he deflated. He was a little boy in a grown-up body—a little boy who felt lost and alone, scared at the depth of his feelings.

Just like me.

He sat on the grass next to me, then lay down on his back and stared up at the sky.

"Macie's right, you know," he said quietly.

"About what?" I asked.

"There's nothing that's going to come of these depositions. There's nothing to pin on Macie. She had everyone else do her dirty work."

I thought about this, and it made my stomach hurt. I suddenly wished that I could push a fast-forward button—that I could make the rest of senior year just speed toward the end, right past graduation, and the summer, and packing. All I wanted was to be a freshman in college someplace, anyplace, where all I had to do was take Comp I and work on a new floor routine.

Jake sat up and looked at me. "I tried to tell her once that it wouldn't matter in ten years," he said.

I had to look away from his gaze. His eyes were too deep with sadness.

"It's not just my fault, or your fault, or even Macie's fault," he said slowly. "It's Leslie's fault too. She could have trusted us to love her."

He looked at me for a moment, then kicked at the loose dirt on top of Leslie's grave. "Do me a favor, Beth."

"Yeah?" I asked.

"The next time you meet a beautiful girl, and she turns you down, will you please be her friend? Leslie Gatlin deserved better. She deserved to be more important to you than Macie Merrick. She deserved—"

His voice cracked, and he bit his lip.

"Someone like you," I said softly. "She deserved someone like you."

"I don't know which is worse," he said. "Feeling guilty or feeling angry for feeling guilty. I'm just not sure which feeling is right."

"Maybe they're both right," I said. "Maybe we're just supposed to feel everything as it comes."

"I'd rather feel happy," said Jake. "I'd rather have Leslie alive."

He looked at his watch and turned toward the parking lot.

"Where are you going?" I asked.

"I've got a deposition," he said.

28. JAKE

The blonde from Brad's house was standing in front of me again. This time her hand was raised, and there was no smirk to be found.

"Do you swear to tell the truth, the whole truth, and nothing but the truth?"

Nothing but the truth. The phrase rang in my ears and I wondered what Macie said when she sat at this shiny table.

"I do," I said.

Then she turned to Jillian. I watched as Jillian raised her right hand and swore to be honest. I hoped that she would be, no matter how hard the questions became. She knew better than to try anything with me sitting here next to her.

Jillian sat down, and instead of asking her a question, Kellan Dirkson turned to me.

"Please state your name for the record," he said. His tone

was clipped and short. He wasn't even looking at me, just leafing through a file on the table.

"Jacob Walker," I said.

"What is your relationship to Leslie Gatlin?"

"I'm her . . . ," I started, but somehow I didn't know how to finish. What was my relationship to Leslie Gatlin? What was I doing here? What was her relationship to me? I had just sworn to tell the truth—the whole truth. The whole room seemed to zoom in toward my eyes—like in space movies when a ship enters warp speed and the stars blur into streaks. *What am I to Leslie Gatlin?* What was I? I was the guy who wanted her more than anything else in the world—and not just her body or her lips, or her arms around me. I wanted her to feel safe when I held her hand in mine. I wanted her to smile when she heard my name. I wanted to be the one person she could tell anything to.

And in that moment—the second question—I realized I couldn't answer truthfully. Not because I didn't want to, but because I didn't know.

I could say "friend," but it was so much more than that. I was staring right at Kellan, frozen in this instant. If I said "friend," that wasn't honest at all, but I had no idea what to say, because Leslie had taken so long to be honest with me.

"Mr. Walker?" Kellan finally looked up from his papers.

"I am her . . . *was* her . . . ," I stuttered.

"Yes?" He peered at me from behind his rimless glasses.

His eyes were blue, but not ice-cold. This was the blue from the heat at the center of the flame. He was hungry, and seemed to be waiting on my answer to begin devouring me.

"I don't know."

The words tumbled out of my mouth softly and seemed to snap the warp speed of the room into a jerking reverse. Patrick was sitting in the chair between Jillian and me. He swiveled toward me slightly, his head cocked like Brad's beagle, Shamus, when he was waiting for his food.

"I'm sorry, Mr. Walker," Kellan Dirkson sighed. "You appear to be confused. I simply need for you to state for the record what your relationship was to Leslie Gatlin."

I hate it when adults get that bullshit tone—the one that says that they know everything and you know nothing and that they've got something better to be doing or someplace more important to be than right here in this moment dealing with you.

"I'm not confused," I said slowly, trying to tamp down the anger that had crawled up the back of my neck and was beginning to tighten the muscles in my throat. "I just want to answer honestly, and I am not sure how to say what our relationship was."

Kellan blinked at me like a furnace. "Perhaps I can help you narrow that down. Were you dating her? Were you sleeping together? Had you ever met? Were you lab partners? You know, just humor us and pick something. These are not difficult questions."

Lauren Wolinsky took a deep breath and shifted in her seat as she shot Kellan a look. She flipped a strand of hair over her shoulder and scribbled a note on her legal pad before looking back at me, her lips pursed.

"Young man," Kellan said, "if you require me to provide multiple-choice suggestions for each answer I need from you today, this deposition may take quite some time."

For some reason, every frustrating moment of the last three weeks—of the last four years—shot into the center of my stomach and rolled over one another until they thundered into my chest and out of my mouth.

"You fucking asshole! Leslie is dead!"

"Jake!" Jillian and Patrick said it at the same time.

"What?" I shot back at them. Patrick tried to put a hand on my shoulder and I stood up like someone had sent a shock through my ass, pushing the white leather swivel chair with a clang into the glass wall that separated the conference room from the hallway. I leveled a look at Jillian that warned her to stay out of this.

"Mr. Walker," Kellan said loudly, sternly. "Kindly take your seat. Stop acting like a child, and answer the question."

"C'mon, buddy," said Patrick quietly, grabbing my chair, pushing it back toward the table, and putting his hand on my shoulder.

"I'm not your fucking buddy," I said softly. Then I leaned over the table toward Kellan Dirkson. "I am not acting like a child. In fact, I'm not acting at all. I loved Leslie Gatlin. I loved her enough to actually be her friend—even when nobody else would. I came here to tell you what fucking happened to her, not to be talked down to."

Everyone stared at me in silence. I sat down in the chair and rolled back up to the table.

"I was Leslie Gatlin's friend," I said. "But for the record, I was more than that."

"Thank you," said Kellan Dirkson quietly. "I apologize if you felt my tone was condescending."

"I don't care about your tone," I said. "I care about whether you actually want to know why Leslie died."

"That's why we're here, Mr. Walker." Kellan's eyes matched the intensity of the heat in my gaze.

"Then maybe you could act like somebody is dead," I said. "Instead of like you're bored and upset that you're missing happy hour."

Lauren Wolinsky covered her mouth as she coughed for a moment, then gulped a long swallow from a bottle of Fiji water in the center of the table. Kellan Dirkson took a deep breath, eyes trained on a piece of paper on top of a manila folder. When he looked up, he fixed me with a faint smile.

"Mr. Walker, would you kindly tell me when the last time you spoke with Leslie Gatlin was?"

"The night she died," I said.

"According to police reports of the incident, it appears that you were the last person to speak with Miss Gatlin before she died. Where did this conversation take place?"

"At her house," I said.

"How long had it been since you talked to Leslie?" Kellan asked.

"About three months. Maybe four."

"Mr. Walker, you just finished telling us that you 'loved' Miss Gatlin." Kellan's eyes sparked. "Why hadn't you talked to her in three or four months?"

"She didn't want to be with me."

"So you stopped talking to her?"

I swallowed hard. I felt like someone had kicked me in the gut. "It was too hard," I said.

"So how is it that you decided to show up on the night before she was found dead in her garage?" When I met Kellan's eyes, he leaned back in his chair and crossed his arms.

"We're waiting, Mr. Walker."

"Someone left Leslie's necklace on the pillow in my bedroom the night before she died," I said.

"Her necklace?" asked Kellan. "How did you know it was hers?"

"Because Jillian and I were with her when she bought it. We all bought necklaces together."

"How did Leslie's necklace end up in your bedroom, Mr. Walker?"

"Macie Merrick put it there."

"How do you know that?" asked Kellan.

"There was a note in Macie's handwriting with the necklace."

"What did the note say?" asked Kellan.

"It said, 'If I can't have what I want, you can't have what you want.'"

"What do you think the note referred to, Jake?"

"Macie was always upset at Leslie because I wanted to go out with Leslie and not with her."

"Did you see Miss Merrick leave the note and the necklace?" asked Kellan.

"No," I said.

"So you found the necklace and decided to go to Leslie's house?" Kellan was making a note on a legal pad.

"Yes," I said. "The necklace was hers, and I wanted to return it."

"You must've had a great deal to catch up on after not speaking for three or four months," Kellan said. "Especially since you loved her and all."

I looked toward the sky outside the conference room windows. I could see the Space Needle from here, and I wanted to be standing on top of it with the wind in my hair. I wanted to be far away from this room and Kellan Dirkson.

Suddenly an image of Leslie flashed into my brain. We were partners for the leaf collection we had to do in biology our sophomore year. I pictured her laughing as we traipsed around the Bloedel Reserve picking up leaves and snapping pictures of the information plaques with our phones.

I remembered sitting next to her on the bench at the edge of the Reflection Pool. The air was cool and moist. She was chilly and I'd put my arm around her as she pulled her jacket closer. There was no one else there inside the hedge that ringed the long, square pool of still water. It was so peaceful. Leslie had taken a deep breath and turned her face up toward the sky. It was overcast but bright—no rain—and the light bouncing off the water almost seemed to make her glow.

I wanted to keep this picture of Leslie in my mind. I wanted to remember her always alive, and fresh, and lit up with the possibility of one more deep breath.

Instead I was here with Kellan Dirkson, being reminded of all the ways I had failed her.

"Yes," I said quietly. "Leslie and I had plenty to talk about."

"Please, enlighten us," said Kellan. "We'd love to hear all about it."

As I walked up the steps at Leslie's front door, I knew I couldn't ring the doorbell and wake up her parents. I texted her:

`Dude. At your front door.`

Finally, she opened it. Something was different. Was it her eyes? I'd almost forgotten how beautiful she was, but something was wrong.

"Jake? What's going on?"

"You tell me," I said, and reached for the necklace in my pocket. I stopped. Leslie was holding a duffel bag.

"Where are you going?" I asked.

"Portland."

"What? Tonight?"

"Shhhh," she said. "Mom just went to bed."

"You're driving there tonight?" I asked again.

"Yeah," she said. She seemed sort of afraid, sad even.

"When are you coming back?" I asked, and as I did, I felt a strange drop in my stomach. *She's not telling you everything.*

"I'm just staying with my aunt Laura for a while. I have to get out of here."

"I'm coming with you," I said.

"It'll just be easier if you're not involved, Jake."

"But I am involved."

She sighed and looked down at the floor. I hooked a finger under her chin and gently pulled it up toward my face. One more time I leaned in close to her. One more time I tried to kiss her. One more time she pulled away.

"Jake, don't."

I stepped back and shook my head. "I don't get you."

"I know," she said.

"What's wrong with me?"

"Nothing, Jake. Everything is right with you."

"Then why won't you kiss me?"

She didn't have an answer. She never did. I remembered

the necklace and pulled it out of my pocket. When she saw it, she frowned and took it from me.

"How did you get this?" she asked.

"Macie left it on my pillow tonight," I said. "The wolf pack is all over at my place with Jillian."

She turned the tiny silver anchor around and around in her palm, like she was looking for some sign, an answer, the missing piece.

"Leslie, why did Macie Merrick have this necklace?"

"I'm not sure," she said, and it was only then I realized she was crying.

"Did you know it was missing? Did she steal it from you?"

"Jake, you have to go."

"Why won't you talk to me?" I asked. She was shutting me out. "Look, I'm so sorry that I haven't been in touch as much since that night at Scarecrow."

"Shh!" She smiled and reached up to place a finger against my lips. "It's okay," she said. "I'm not upset with you. It's just that nobody can stop what's been going on except me. Not even you. Go home. I have to get going."

"Why are you being like this?" A pulse of anger surged through me.

Leslie looked up at me with tired eyes. "Jake, I'm sorry. I just need a break from the whole thing with Macie."

"And me, I guess?" The words flew out of my mouth before I could stop them.

She shrugged and nodded.

I paused on the front porch and turned back to her.

"Remember that night on the beach in Cape Cod, right before our freshman year?"

"Jake, please don't be angry with me." She had tears in her eyes.

"What happened to that girl?"

Leslie looked down at the necklace in her hand. Tears streamed down her cheeks. "She's gone, Jake. Sometimes I don't know if she ever existed."

My frustration boiled over. "She did exist, Leslie. I remember her. She never shut me out like this."

"You should leave now," Leslie said softly.

There were so many words I wanted to say, but Leslie stepped back and filled the widening silence between us with two:

"Good-bye, Jake."

Then she closed the door and left me standing on the porch. Alone.

"So why didn't Leslie Gatlin make it to Portland?" Kellan Dirkson was shuffling papers again.

"I don't know," I said softly. "I was one of the last people to find out."

Kellan had three pieces of white paper, which he passed to Jillian, then Patrick, then me. "Maybe the email you sent

Miss Gatlin after you left her house that night had something to do with it?"

I frowned at him, then looked down at the page.

In front of me was a printout of an email. It had been sent from my email account.

Leslie,

I'm tired of you turning me down. You don't deserve somebody like me. You are pathetic and worthless. Maybe Macie is right. You should just kill yourself.
Done trying,

Jake

Suddenly I couldn't breathe, and slowly the letters on the page blurred in front of me. I was crying. I stood up, stumbling over the chair behind me as I backed away from the piece of paper that lay on the glossy white table. Kellan was asking me something, calling me Mr. Walker. Patrick was telling me to sit down and objecting about something. Jillian sat next to him, staring at the page in front of her, as white as the paper and the table and the chairs in the room. When she looked up at me, I knew.

"You?" I gasped. "You did this?"

She slowly stood up, and in the midst of Kellan's shuffling and Patrick's objecting, all I could see was Jillian, looking toward me as I approached her. She was terrified. She was guilty.

"Please, Jake." Her voice was coming from tin speakers someplace far below me. "Please! I didn't—"

"How could you do this to me?" I choked out.

I heard Kellan's voice shatter the blaze in my brain. "Mr. Walker. Have you ever seen this email before?"

"*No!*" I roared back at him.

"Miss Walker, did you send this email from Jacob's account?"

Jillian stared at the table and shook her head.

"You gave her my computer, didn't you?" I knew the answer even before Jillian looked at me and said, "Yes."

She may have said more. She certainly did, but I didn't hear it. I had reached the door to the conference room and was sprinting down the hall, past Katherine's father, past a secretary walking across the hallway toward her desk, her white earbuds draped around her neck.

I burst through the doors of the building like I was coming up for air. There was a grassy area next to the fountains that lined the walkway out front. I raced toward the patch of lawn as I felt myself fall, and when my knees hit the soft, moist green, I wished that it would open up and swallow me whole.

29. JILLIAN

When Jake tore out of the room, Patrick strode toward the door like he was going to chase him down, then stopped, reached one hand out, and leaned against the glass wall of the conference room. His head dropped. He stared at his shoes for a moment, then he slowly walked back over to his chair and collapsed into it.

"Sit," he said to me, and with one hand he reached out and grabbed my chair, rolling it back toward the table. I sat.

Kellan took off his glasses and pinched the bridge of his nose with his thumb and forefinger. When he replaced them, he glanced at Lauren Wolinsky, who was staring at me without a smile.

"Just one question," Kellan said. "Miss Walker, did you send this email from Jacob's account to Leslie Gatlin?"

"No," I said.

In the silence that followed, Lauren Wolinsky shifted forward in her chair across the table from me. She slowly leaned across the table, folded her hands, and stared directly into my eyes.

"Then who did?" she asked. Her gaze cut right through me. "And remember, Miss Walker, you are under oath."

I'll never forget how we sat there in silence for what seemed like an eternity as we listened to the front door slam, then the car door, then heard Jake squeal away from the curb. And in the span of time between his tires peeling out and Krista's next giggle, I sat in the silence and understood two things:

I didn't know exactly how we'd gotten here.

But I knew exactly where Jake was going: He was headed to Leslie's.

"Jesus," said Krista, picking up the lamp and placing it back on the dresser. "Jake is such a spaz."

"He just needs the right girl to channel all that pent-up energy toward," said Macie with an arched eyebrow. "God, Jills. You'd think after all this time you could help me wear him down a little."

"Macie. You know Jake," I said. "He's never done anything he doesn't want to."

"Or anyone." Krista snickered.

Katherine rolled her eyes as she blew her nails dry.

"What?" Krista asked.

"That boy just needs to get out more," Katherine said. "He

needs to see that there is more than just this one cloudy corner of the world."

"So true, VP," said Macie. "So very, very true. Maybe I'll just kidnap that boy and take him to Paris next summer." When she said it, she was looking at me, and in short order, everyone was looking at her.

"Paris?" asked Beth. "You're going to Paris?"

Macie smirked. "It's true. The senator promised me a trip for graduation, and even better than that . . ." She paused for effect. "I get a plus one."

"Oh. Em. Geeeeee," squealed Krista. "Take me, take me, take me!"

My stomach started to drop. Macie had called me about this trip the minute she'd found out at Christmastime. "Pack your bags, *mon chéri*," she'd purred into the phone. "We're heading to the continent." She'd sworn me to secrecy about it so that no one else would get jealous. We'd been planning for months.

"Who are you taking? Who are you taking?" Krista was on her knees, bouncing up and down on my bed, about to have a cardiac arrest.

"Well . . . ," Macie said, looking directly at me. "I haven't decided yet."

"What?" I said, and before I realized the word had fallen out of my mouth, Macie smirked and turned to the rest of the room.

"Keep your schedules open, ladies. I'll need a friend in Paris. I'll decide by graduation."

I actually felt dizzy. I had already been shopping for the trip. I felt my heart race. I could hear the pounding in my ears.

Beth was back at the computer on my desk, already looking at the hotel Macie was telling them her dad had booked. Krista was squawking and pointing and shrieking; Beth was wide-eyed and smiling; even Katherine was drinking in the pictures over Beth's shoulder.

Macie turned to me with an innocent smile. "Jillian, go grab the laptop and pull up that email I sent you with the exact dates."

"I don't know where it is," I said.

"Oh, please." She rolled her eyes. "It's in Jake's room. I saw it in there when I left him the necklace."

I stared at her hard. Hadn't I learned that she was like this when I came back from vacation two years ago and she introduced me to Katherine as her new VP candidate? I walked out of my bedroom and into Jake's. I saw the laptop sitting on his bed. I clicked the enter key, and the screen jumped to life.

Numbly, I clicked open a new tab on the browser and typed in "gmail.com," but instead of a log-in page, I saw an in-box load. I blinked. It was Jake's in-box.

Jake and I had shared this MacBook for the past year. I inherited Dad's old PC desktop when school started, and Jake had convinced Mom and Dad to get us the laptop so that he

didn't have to sit in my room to do homework. We both had a user account set up on the laptop, and in all the months we'd passed it back and forth, I had never once powered it on to find that Jake was still signed in. He always signed out when he was done. Always.

As I was staring at his Gmail in-box, I heard a voice behind me.

"Find it?" Macie asked. I whipped my head around and saw her standing in the doorway of Jake's room with her arms crossed.

I looked back at the screen, and my heart started pounding. I looked back at her.

"No. I found something else," I said flatly.

"Oh, really?" she asked. "Did Jake leave an XTube video open?" She giggled.

"You know, you can be a real bitch," I shot at her.

Both of her eyebrows shot up as she surveyed my face. Then she threw her head back and laughed. "Oh, please, Jills. You're not really upset about this Paris thing, are you?"

"You said we were going together—just us," I said.

"Well, that's hardly fair to anyone else, is it?" she said with a glare.

"When have you ever been worried about what's fair?" I asked.

"Nothing wrong with a little friendly competition, is there?" She was so pleased with herself. That smug, self-satisfied smil

on her face made me so furious, the top of my head felt hot under my hair.

"Oh, so now I have to *compete* to be a better friend to you?" I was almost shouting.

"Why not?" asked Macie with her imperial ice-queen voice. "What do you have to offer me, Jillian? Why should I take you with me?"

Her voice stopped me cold. It was like the cold slap of the ocean water against my face that summer in Cape Cod. Macie Merrick was looking at me and all she could see was the person I saw when I looked in the mirror. The answer to her question rang in my ears: *Nothing. I have nothing to offer you.*

I couldn't look at her anymore. My gaze fell back down to the screen, and when it did, I realized I was wrong.

My fingers were shaking as I moved the cursor across the in-box. I could hear something inside me—the voice of an old friend from far away: *Don't do this*, it said. *This is not who you are.* I paused with my finger on the trackpad—the cursor hovered just over the "log out" link in the upper-right corner. One click, and the moment would be over—the possibility would pass. And so would my trip to Europe. The voice in my head seemed to grow more and more faint. I turned to look at Macie again, and something about her gaze made the voice fade away completely.

"What would you say if I offered you complete access to Jake's email account?" I asked. I spun the laptop around on my lap so that she could see the screen. She glanced from me to the screen and then back to me again.

"You're shitting me," she whispered.

I arched an eyebrow and shook my head. "What's that worth to you?" I asked.

Slowly, Macie Merrick crossed the room staring at the screen on my lap and slumped onto the bed to see for herself.

"That," she whispered, "is worth a first-class ticket to Charles de Gaulle."

Then she moved the cursor slowly across the screen, away from "log out," and clicked Compose.

I slid off the bed and headed to the door of Jake's room.

"Where are you going?" she asked.

"Paris," I said.

Then I walked back to my room as I heard Macie start to type.

After what seemed like hours, Kellan Dirkson finally said, "No further questions," and Patrick said something I don't remember, and then I was walking down the long hallway and out of the building.

When I got to Jake's car, he was already there, buckled in. He stared straight ahead when I slid into the passenger seat. His eyes were swollen from crying, and his face was red and blotchy.

"Don't talk to me."

"Jake, it's not what you think—"

"It is, Jillian. It is what I think," he said quietly.

"I didn't know what she was going to write," I said.

He turned and looked at me and smiled bitterly. "Sure you did, Jillian."

"I didn't know that—"

"Stop. Talking. Now."

Jake's voice was so quiet and so ferocious that I was scared. His knuckles were white on the steering wheel as he drove us home in complete silence. When we pulled up in front of the house, I saw Mom and Dad were both already home. Mom had promised us steaks on the grill tonight. She and Dad would want to know all about the deposition. We'd have to relive this one more time. Jake was staring at their cars too when I glanced at him. I knew he was thinking the same thing.

Suddenly I was crying. I was so exhausted. I didn't want to talk about Macie or Leslie or anything anymore. I just wanted us to go inside and sit down with Mom and Dad and laugh and smile and know that everything was going to be okay.

"I'm so sorry, Jake," I whispered.

He stared out the window at our house and the cars in the driveway. The sun had dropped below the clouds and was shooting flames off the snow on Mount Hood; dark-magenta rays spread across the sky. Any other night it would have been beautiful.

"Let me spell this out for you," he said without looking at

me. "We will live here together until the end of the summer. We will go to college, and we may even see each other over breaks and at Christmas, but you are not my sister anymore."

"Jake, please—"

He held up his hand. "You are actually worse than Macie Merrick, Jillian." He tried to go on, but his voice cracked, and he had to stop and swallow. "Macie hated Leslie from day one. But not you—you were actually her friend once. You're worse because you turned your back on Leslie. You knew that this was wrong, and you went along with it anyway. Every step."

"Jake, I just want to explain it to you." The tears were hot on my cheeks, and my chest shook. I could barely form the words.

Jake took off his seat belt and shook his head.

"You could talk from now until the end of time, Jillian, and there'd still be no explanation for this," he said. "I'm done talking to you, and I'm done listening to you. I never want to hear you say another word."

30. KATHERINE

"Daysun—this is hopeless. I want to prosecute these girls myself."

Patrick's voice was strained and angry. I couldn't blame him. His week had been ten kinds of torment. After my deposition on Monday, Macie's had followed on Tuesday before Jillian and Jake's crash-and-burn disaster Friday.

I slipped off the couch in Daddy's reception area and listened. The door of his office was partly open. It was Saturday afternoon. Daddy had played tennis with his doubles partner early this morning, and then come into the office to tie up some loose ends on the permitting case. I'd come with him to study for my chemistry exam on Monday in the peace and quiet of the empty firm, but when we walked in Patrick was pacing the hall outside Daddy's office.

"I'm serious, Daysun. I'm ready to switch sides in this case."

"Patrick, please." Daddy's voice was slow and low. "I know this has been hard, but we don't have to prove anything here. Burden of proof is on the prosecution. They've got to show that there was some sort of responsibility here. And no one has ever been proven guilty of causing someone else's suicide."

Through the space between the door and its frame I saw Patrick place his hands wide on Daddy's desk and lean across the dark mahogany. "Daysun, they are responsible for this suicide. Every one of them."

When I heard Patrick say this, I remembered walking down the hallway with Daddy on Tuesday afternoon. Mike Merrick had rounded the corner, with Macie, clicking along behind him.

When her dad stopped to shake hands with mine, Macie leveled her eyes at me but didn't speak.

"How'd it go in there, Senator?" Daddy boomed, pumping his hand.

"Just fine, Daysun. Just fine." Mike Merrick was smiling like a possum eating briars. Or at least that's what Aunt Liza would say. "Just can't thank you and Patrick enough for prepping the kids so well on this."

"Happy to help." Daddy smiled. "Just got back from some tennis at the Bellevue Club. Let's schedule a match when this is all over."

"You've got yourself a deal," he said and smiled, all charm and teeth and tan.

Macie raised her eyebrows at me and let out a long sigh as if to say she were bored. As her dad held the front door open for her, she turned back to look at me and narrowed her eyes. Then she stepped out the door and slipped her sunglasses onto her face like she was avoiding a group of paparazzi, and walked with her father toward the parking deck.

Something about this memory and the sound of the anger in Patrick's voice made me feel like I was falling. I steadied myself on the doorframe as Daddy eyed Patrick wearily.

"These are not bad kids," Daddy said. "You remember high school. It all seems very important, and let's face it: Kids are kids. They include some and exclude others. That's just evolution. You gather your pack and you survive because of safety in numbers. Leslie Gatlin had her pack just as sure as Macie and Katherine did."

"Leslie had no pack, Daysun."

Daddy was quiet for a moment, then said, "Okay, Patrick. So let's say for a second that you're right. Let's say that the evidence here points to wrongful death. What does Kellan Dirkson say that he's gonna charge Macie Merrick with?"

"That's just it," sighed Patrick. "Macie Merrick can't be charged with civil liability in this case. She's the only one who didn't actually do anything that can be proven. You should've seen her in that deposition. She was perfect. An ice queen with a warm smile. That girl is the best liar I've ever seen."

"She perjured herself?" Daddy's voice was sharp.

"She didn't have to. She got everybody else to do her dirty work. The one email I'm sure she sent was forged from Jacob Walker's account—on his laptop. There's no way to prove that she wrote it, and she knows it. So does her dad."

Patrick was quiet for a moment. "Daysun, this civil case is over. We won, and Dirkson knows it. There's a single instance in Massachusetts where criminal charges were brought in a suicide case, and that's been tied up in paperwork for months. There's just not enough legal precedent to bring a criminal case here."

"So what are you so worked up about?" Daddy asked. "You won."

"Then why does it feel like I lost?" Patrick asked quietly.

"The purpose of the law is handin' out justice, Patrick, not warm, fuzzy feelings."

Patrick stood up and put his hands in the pockets of his flat-front chinos and looked at the toes of his spit-shined penny loafers. "So how does Leslie Gatlin get her justice?" he asked quietly.

My daddy has made a career of having an answer every time somebody asks him a question. As long as I can remember, folks have been asking Daddy for advice—not just about the law but about everything. Aunt Liza used to say that when God was handin' out smarts, Daddy was first in line and came back for seconds.

For the first time in the seventeen years I had known him,

my daddy answered a question with a deafening silence: There would be no justice for Leslie Gatlin.

Patrick got the quiet answer loud and clear, and turned toward the door without looking up from his shoes. I slipped back onto the couch and opened my chemistry book. When he walked into the foyer, Patrick paused and looked up at me. I held his gaze for a moment, then he shook his head and walked out the door.

I sat in the silence for a moment, then I closed my chem book again and silently walked into Daddy's office. He was sitting at his desk looking at a picture in a silver frame that he'd always kept next to his computer in every office he'd ever had.

It was a picture Aunt Liza snapped of me wearin' Mama's high heels when I was three years old.

He didn't look up. He just sat and stared at the picture. When he spoke, he didn't move his eyes away from the frame.

"I wonder what it's like?" he said softly.

"What?" I asked.

"Knowin' that the little girl you loved for all those years was downstairs, dead in the garage while you were sleepin'." There were tears running down his cheeks—something else I had never witnessed in my entire life.

"Patrick's right," I said softly, my eyes flooding over like a bathtub with the water running. "It was our fault, Daddy." I sank onto the leather chair opposite his desk and buried my face in my hands. "Can you ever forgive me?" I sobbed.

Then I felt his arms around me, in a wordless grip so tight that I cried even harder—his second silent answer of the day.

When I had cried myself dry against his shoulder, Daddy reached into his back pocket and handed me a crisp linen handkerchief.

"Katherine," he said. "I have recused myself from this case because you are my daughter, but it appears that this case is now over." He stood up and walked to his desk. He sat back in his chair and swiveled sideways to look out the window at the gathering clouds in the afternoon sky. The light was beautiful and his skin glowed the same deep brown as his desk. There was a glint in his eyes when he asked me, "Have you watched all the depositions?"

"I've seen them all," I said. "Except Macie's."

"From what I understand, that swim team captain—what's his name? Dating the Braddock girl?"

"Josh Phillips?" I asked.

"Does he really have that video of Marty Merrick?"

"Yes, sir," I said.

Daddy pressed the tips of his fingers together, then tapped them against each other while he stared out the window. "Kathy, I'm going to ask you something, and I want the God's honest truth from you, young lady."

He swung around in his chair and faced me dead-on. I nodded.

"If the DA were to file criminal charges against Macie

Merrick, would Jillian and Beth testify against her? On the stand? Under oath?"

"Yes, sir," I said. "But, Daddy—won't you just run into the same problem with not being able to pin anything on Macie? The evidence is circumstantial, isn't it? It's our word against hers. How are you going to prove anything?"

"Oh, I'm not gonna be proving anything, sweetheart." He was dialing his phone. "Yes, hello. This is Daysun Fraisure calling. Is District Attorney Braddock available?" He covered the mouthpiece with his hand.

"You're sure about Jillian and Beth?" he whispered.

I raised my right hand. "I swear."

31. BETH

Sitting across the table from District Attorney Graham Braddock, it was hard not to feel like I was in trouble. I kept making lists of all the reasons I shouldn't be afraid:

1. Katherine's dad was going to do all the talking.
2. Jillian and Katherine were here with me.
3. Macie didn't know what we were doing. Yet.

When we got back to school and slid into third period, Macie didn't bat an eye. She wasn't really speaking to any of us anymore anyway. Krista was a different story. She kept turning around and staring, making faces, narrowing her eyes, passing notes to Macie, laughing. It was almost comical.

She kept at it all day, but it was easier to ignore her than I had expected it would be because I had Katherine and Jillian to walk to classes and eat with. We didn't say much. We were just there for one another.

I couldn't help but think that maybe if we'd all just been there for one another sooner, Leslie would still be alive.

And that was a thought I couldn't get out of my head. It kept getting louder throughout the afternoon, until it was all I could hear. By the time I got to practice, the volume was turned up to eleven, and as I was opening the first handspring of my third tumbling pass into a full layout, I knew I was going to land out of bounds.

Again.

I'd been running this floor routine the entire practice. The momentum of a tumbling pass that you've done about a thousand times in the past three months is a very specific thing. Nailing a double back layout with a twist is something I'd never done in a competition before, and this week I hadn't even done it in practice. I nailed the landing and stepped back, and before my heel had even landed a full foot past the bounding line, I could see Coach Stevens's clipboard flying into the bleachers.

"That's it!" His voice echoed across the gym. "Circle up!"

I felt like I had bricks tied to my ankles as I trudged across the gym to the huddle. I felt like I had as I'd climbed the stairs to the DA's office this morning. It's one thing to give a deposition. It's another thing to sit in a room with a criminal prosecutor and a lawyer and hear the strategy for filing criminal charges against Macie Merrick.

As the other girls on the team ran in to Coach Stevens, he stood there, hands on his hips, silently shaking his head. He didn't need to yell. He knew I knew. I jumped a couple of times on the spring floor, trying to shake it off. Then I slowly walked over to where he stood in the semicircle, dismissing the other girls.

"One week, team. I need your bodies here, but more importantly, I need your *brains in the game.* If your head isn't here, you might as well keep your tricks in your trunk. It's not enough to just do a routine—even a clean routine. I need your concentration and your focus. If you think Woodinville is going to show up to this meet and just hand over their four-year championship streak, you've got another thought coming."

He looked down at the mat he was standing on, then back up with a smile. "When you guys bring your brains, you're unbeatable. See you tomorrow."

I didn't even turn around to head to the locker room. I knew better. I knew he'd want a word with me. I closed my eyes and took a deep breath. I knew it was coming.

But it didn't.

When I didn't hear Coach lay into me about the floor routine, I looked up and saw him climbing out of the bleachers where he'd retrieved his clipboard. Then he turned and started walking toward his office.

"Coach?" I asked. My voice seemed tiny in the empty gym.

He stopped but didn't turn around. "Yeah, Beth?"

"Do I need to . . . Should I . . ." What was I asking?

He turned around and crossed his arms over his chest and looked at me. "Should you what?" His voice was tired.

"I don't know . . . I just . . ." It felt like I should be talking to him about something. I wasn't sure it was gymnastics. "What should I do?" I asked.

"About what?" he asked.

I had no answer. I didn't know where to start. I wasn't sure what to do about anything. The doubt and lies and exhaustion of the past month came crashing onto me all at once. I felt like I was pinned to the floor by the silence. The air between us was thick with everything I couldn't say. After a moment Coach shook his head.

"Go home, Beth. Or wherever it is that you go when you're not here. Go there, and if you have a moment, think about what you've been doing here in practice all week. Think about how close you are, and then think about why you're about to fumble the best floor routine you've ever put together at the meet next week."

My eyes stung as he turned around and headed back toward his office.

"I'm sorry," I whispered, wiping at my cheeks. I couldn't believe he heard me, but he stopped in his tracks and turned around to face me. He stared at me for what seemed like an eternity, and then nodded slowly, his lips pursed together.

"Me too, Beth," he said. "Me too."

• • •

I left school and drove without thinking where I was going. I wound up parking across the street from Leslie's house and staring at the garage door. I wondered what it must have been like for her that night. I wondered what it must be like for her family now.

As I sat there staring at her house, the garage door opened, and Mrs. Gatlin followed Mr. Gatlin into the front yard. She was holding a glass of white wine. He was holding a mallet and a For Sale sign, which he drove into the ground by the mailbox.

Before I realized what was happening, I had opened my car door and was walking across the street toward them in a daze.

"Beth?" Mrs. Gatlin stared at me with wide, glassy eyes.

The three of us stood there in silence, staring at one another.

"What are you doing here?" Mr. Gatlin asked.

"I don't know, exactly," I said. "I guess, I just wanted to say I'm sorry."

Mr. Gatlin turned back toward the house and silently walked up the stairs to the front door. My cheeks burned at his silent dismissal. *What am I doing here?* I turned to leave.

"Beth?" Mrs. Gatlin's voice stopped me, and I turned around.

"Yes?" I asked.

"I . . . I just wanted to let you know how much I appreciate what you girls did this morning, going in to meet with Mr. Braddock. I know it wasn't easy."

I sighed and nodded at her.

"Where are you moving this time?" I asked, nodding at the sign in the yard.

"We're headed to Florida."

"Florida?" I asked.

"Yes," she said softly. "Time to go somewhere warm. I've had enough of this rain."

"But . . . what about the criminal case?" I asked. "You'll be back to testify, right?"

"Oh—" She paused and looked back at me. "We've decided not to pursue it," she said, and leaned against the For Sale sign as if she hoped it would hold her up.

"What?" I couldn't believe I had heard her. "But we just met with the DA this morning—"

"Mr. Gatlin has a project going on here," she said. "It's a big development and it has been delayed in permitting and environmental studies with the state for over three years. If we don't get the permits approved now, the investors will pull out."

I didn't understand. Something was wrong here. "But . . . what does that have to do with . . ."

"Leslie?" she asked. When I was silent, she smiled at me like I was a little girl who just didn't understand.

"Mr. Merrick came over this morning while you girls were meeting with the DA," she explained. "He told Glen that if we refused to participate in the case, the DA wouldn't be able to proceed, and that if we agreed not take this any further, he'd have our permits approved this afternoon."

Anger swelled into my chest and burst out in a torrent of tears and words that I couldn't control.

"But why wouldn't you want this to go to court?" I gasped.

She looked around at the yard, as if she just couldn't bear to see any more tears. She sighed deeply, like she was letting something go.

"Putting Macie Merrick on trial won't make anything better."

"Maybe not," I said. "But letting her get away with this makes everything worse."

32. JAKE

They were already digging foundations by the time I had the guts to go see the place. Yesterday Beth had called me in hysterics from the curb in front of the Gatlins' place. Today, Glen Gatlin was pacing back and forth monitoring his new development: seventeen thousand square feet of multipurpose retail stores and condominiums, with live/work loft spaces and two big-box stores.

"There he is," I said as I spotted Leslie's dad.

"Want me to come with you?" Brad asked.

"Nah. I got this." I slid out of his truck. "Back in a flash," I said, and closed the door. Then I strode across the packed dirt toward Mr. Gatlin.

I fell into step with Mr. Gatlin and a foreman in a hard hat as they walked toward the closest building.

"Mr. Gatlin?"

He turned and stopped short when he saw me.

"Got a second?" I asked, putting a hand out. He didn't take it, but didn't turn away.

"Gimme a second, Jim?" he asked without taking his eyes off mine.

"Sure thing." The foreman nodded at me and headed on toward the site.

"Can I help you, Jake?"

"Hope so," I said. "Just need a minute of your time."

"What kind of help you looking for?" he asked.

"Help understanding something," I said.

He took off his cap and ran a hand through his hair, then replaced it, looking back at me hard. "What's that?"

"How you could trade justice for money?" I said.

"I don't think I like your tone," he said. "You don't know anything about me."

"I know your daughter thought you were a pretty amazing guy," I said. "She used to tell me all the time."

He shook his head and chuckled quietly to himself, then looked back at me. "Guess she was wrong," he said. "Turns out she was wrong about a couple things."

"Like what?" I asked.

His eyes narrowed. "Like what a smart kid you were, for one. You weren't the only one she talked to all the time, Jake. Fact is, you weren't around much at all those last few months."

His words felt like a kick in the gut, and he must've seen it on my face.

"Aw, c'mon, Jake. Let's not make it like this. I know you're a good kid. I know you mean well, but you can't fight a force like Mike Merrick."

I looked out at the vast expanse that would soon be buildings and parking lots and, at the end of the day, a paycheck. "So if you can't lick 'em, join 'em, huh? Or at least get what you want."

Mr. Gatlin walked over to me and surveyed the construction site. I felt him put an arm around my shoulders. "Bad business won't bring Leslie back."

I shook his arm off and headed toward Brad's truck.

33. JILLIAN

I took tulips because I wasn't sure what was appropriate. Roses felt like something a boyfriend should bring, and the daisies at the place where I stopped looked really picked over. The tulips were bulbs in a pot, and the guy at the shop said that they might actually sprout again next year if I put them in the ground. He was cute, and when I told him I was going to a grave, he let me borrow a spade as long as I promised to bring it back before they closed.

Who does that? Let's you borrow a spade?

So I got to the cemetery and I dug a little hole. Then I gently pulled at the base of the tulips, wiggling them slowly back and forth until I had worked the whole dirt clump out of the pot. I placed it carefully into the hole and pressed the dirt back into it with the spade.

The headstone that Leslie's parents had chosen was about

three feet tall and smooth granite. Nothing rough-hewn—it was all sleek lines and clean edges. And as I sat and looked at it, I thought about how it was so unlike the way she lived and died. There had been no clean edges for Leslie's life, no solid lines, nothing sleek. It had been rough and messy—full of ups and mainly downs and a lot of broken hearts.

This was the first time I'd been to see her grave. I thought about writing a note to her, or preparing something to say to her, but it just felt silly.

Katherine thought that Leslie was in heaven. She'd said so in her op-ed for the *Westport Star*, our school paper. She'd caused a big stir last week when she wrote an open letter of confession for her part in bullying Leslie Gatlin. She told the whole story, named names, and resigned from her position as student council vice president. Macie was furious.

Macie had immediately called for new elections so that she could get Krista installed as the new VP, but Principal Jenkins actually put his foot down and appointed Kelly from the volleyball team. Macie was furious.

Macie was angriest with me. When she'd found out that Katherine and Beth and I had agreed to testify against her in the event of a criminal trial, she'd stopped talking to all three of us immediately. Almost instantly, two new junior girls who wore too much makeup started following her everywhere.

Beth Patterson had been sick to her stomach the morning of the state competition, but decided to perform anyway. She stepped out of bounds on three of her four tumbling passes, and earned her lowest score in three seasons. She's started attending Gay-Straight Alliance meetings. Katherine and I have started going with her.

Of course, this makes Macie even more furious.

But it's made the rest of us free.

It's a strange thing when you spend so much time and energy fearing the worst will happen. Turns out that when it finally occurs, it's pretty much as bad as you thought it would be. In fact, some parts are worse. Then an amazing thing happens.

You see clearly for the first time what made the terrible thing so frightening in the first place: You didn't think you'd survive.

But you do. Or at least I did.

I sat at the grave and looked at the orange tulips against that clean-edged gravestone and wondered why Leslie didn't survive.

I don't understand what makes you lose hope. What was the moment when Leslie decided to walk toward the garage? What makes the difference between the choice to move forward and the choice to stop choosing forever?

I thought about asking the question out loud, actually talking to Leslie, but I couldn't. I don't believe she exists anymore. Katherine says that's the saddest thing she's ever heard, and maybe it is. I don't believe she's in heaven—not because I believe she's in hell; I just don't believe in either of those places. Beth says that she thinks Leslie will be reincarnated and come back as something else—though if you press her on the issue, she isn't sure what.

I guess I think that Leslie died. She really died. Her body is in the ground here, and the only place that she lives on is in the memories of those of us who knew her.

So I sat and thought of our trip to Cape Cod four years ago. I remembered how we swam, and laughed, and lay on the beach talking for hours as the waves crashed across the sand.

I wished Leslie was here again, sitting right beside me. I wished she was someplace where she could hear me when I said I was sorry for all the choices I made one way that I wish I'd made another.

I thought it would fix things for Jake and me when I went to the DA with Katherine and Beth, but it didn't. Jake nodded silently when I told him we were going. He said, "I'm glad," then walked down the stairs. Other than that, he hasn't spoken a word to me beyond, "Excuse me," and "Pass the salt, please." I feel like I'm missing something inside, and I don't know how to fix it.

I put the spade into the empty pot and reached up to the chain at my neck. I unhooked the clasp and gently lifted the tiny captain's wheel out of my shirt. Slowly I laid the chain across the top of the headstone. I opened my mouth to try to say something out loud to a girl who couldn't hear me, but suddenly I couldn't speak. There was a knot in my throat, and tears welled up in my eyes.

"I'm sorry, Leslie," I whispered. "I'll never be the same because of what happened. I swear."

I wiped my eyes and reached down to pick up the pot and the spade. I had to get it back to the guy at the shop before six p.m. tonight. I tucked my hair behind my ear and stood up to head back to the parking lot. That's when I turned around and saw Brad.

He was parked at the curb closest to Leslie's grave. He was leaning up against the passenger side of his truck, hands in his jacket pockets. His bangs were blowing into his face, but he didn't move his hand to push them aside.

I stood frozen to the spot for a minute, and then took a deep breath and started slowly toward him. I stopped a few feet away, unsure of what to say. So I just stood there. Waiting.

He looked past me, to the grave. "Haven't been out here yet," he said.

"How'd you find this place?" I asked.

"Jake told me," he said.

I looked back over my shoulder. I could see the orange tulips marking Leslie's plot with a little flame. When I met Brad's gaze again, we stared at each other for a minute that felt like an eternity. Then he blinked up at the brightness. The clouds were big columns of white against electric blue.

"Surprised Jake talked to me at all," said Brad quietly. "We haven't really even hung out since I went with him to see Mr. Gatlin. He still upset with you?"

I had no power over what Leslie had chosen in the past, or what Macie would choose in the future. I couldn't make better choices for either of them, or change the choices I had made before. I could only move forward by making sure the choice I made in this instant was the best one I could possibly make.

I stared at Brad's outstretched hand. I hadn't let myself imagine this moment after he'd told me it was over. He had hurt me too badly. The question now was not one of whether I loved Brad; it was a question of whether Brad had changed.

Do people change? Maybe Macie hadn't, or Krista. I thought of all the things that were different inside me since Leslie's death. When I thought about all that had changed in Katherine and Beth, it gave me the hope that maybe Brad had too. Just enough hope to take a chance.

And take his hand.

"Can we start over?" he whispered.

"No," I said. "But we can keep going."

Then he helped me into his truck, and we drove toward my car in the parking lot.